Eagle Behind
the Curtain

EAGLE BEHIND THE CURTAIN

Published by Nissi Publishing, Inc.
Roanoke, Texas

This is a work of fiction. Names, characters, places and incidents
are either the product of the author's imagination or are used
fictitiously. Any resemblance to actual persons, living or
dead, events or locales is entirely coincidental. The Windecker Eagle
is an actual aircraft, though some characteristics may have been changed.

ISBN - 978-0-944372-18-0

nissibooks.com
eaglebehindthecurtain.com

Eagle Behind the Curtain

David B. Freeman

1

Early Spring 1992

"I've been had," Alex Davis swore under his breath as he reached for the TV remote, knocking it off on the floor. Black and white snow stared at him from the TV screen, signaling the end of the tape. He fumbled for the controller and found it under a chair. Picking it up, Davis clicked off the set angrily. Too late—the damage had already been done. Three strides and Davis was across the floor. He snatched up the phone and dialed a familiar number. It was answered by his business partner on the third ring. "Bud, this is Alex. Where did you get that tape?"

"The videotape comparing Soviet and American radar technology?"

"Of course. What tape do you think I'm talking about?"

"Ken sent it from Washington. Why?"

Davis hung up, leaving Bud Ewing holding a dead receiver. Hearing the dial tone, Ewing started to dial Alex's number. Clicking off suddenly without an explanation was not like

Alex. But it was Sunday afternoon and raining—nap time. Whatever was bothering Alex could wait until Monday morning.

For ten minutes Alex paced the floor of his den. Twice he stopped by the phone, wondering if he should just go ahead and dial the number. He wished Susan was home. He couldn't talk to her about the videotape, but at least he could get it out of his mind for a while. He needed to clear his head, to get a chance to think things through.

He sat down at his personal computer and called up the Tetris IV game. At least the Russians had been good for something during the short-lived warming of relations. This version of Tetris was as good as any computer game Alex had ever tried. He played the game for a few minutes, then suddenly froze, staring at the send and receive data lights on his modem. They weren't blinking. Had they blinked? Was it possible they had gotten to him through his computer system? A virus? Possibly, but the security on Alex's system was tight. And it was always off when he wasn't at home.

Alex exited Windows and turned off the computer. He stood up and scanned the stack of software CDs on the shelf over his desk, looking for something out of place. Over the weekend, he had used the US phone directory, Compton's Encyclopedia and parts of the Microsoft Bookshelf. Not any harm there.

Then it hit him. The Internet—the Information Super Highway. Fascinated by the sheer volume of online services available through the Internet Gateway, Alex had spent hours browsing online through his modem. There would be no more computing for him for a while. He had to get away.

Outside it was raining—a cold, hard, driving rain. March was shaping up to be as bad as February. So much for the idea of taking a walk. Finally, out of frustration, Alex dialed the number. It was a number he had not used in ten years; nevertheless, it was still indelibly etched in his mind. He waited patiently through the switching. Seven rings, then the recording. He waited through the "all circuits are busy, would you please try your call again later" message. At the completion of the third repetition of the message, Alex pressed the four-digit number which had been his code. The procedure seemed natural, familiar—surprising, considering the years that had passed. Must be the tape, Alex surmised. He knew what would happen next. It didn't. Three clicks and the line went dead.

Driving would clear his head, even in the rain. Alex headed for the garage. Because of the dreary weather, the roads were almost deserted. Most of the inhabitants of Alex Davis' North Dallas community had apparently chosen to stay warm and dry at home on this rainy Sunday afternoon. Water splashed on the windshield and the steering wheel was nearly jerked out of Alex's hand as his Jeep Cherokee plowed through puddles of water trapped in the uneven pavement of the suburban streets. Headed no place in particular, Alex drove until he noticed the Jeep's fuel gauge read "empty." How long it had been that way, he had no idea. A 7-Eleven appeared ahead and Alex turned in. He left the Jeep at the gas pumps and ran inside to wait for a break in the downpour.

The convenience store clerk watched the man get out of his Jeep and run toward the store. When he came in, she breathed a quiet sigh of relief. He didn't look like the type that had robbery or rape on his mind. She was alone in the store, had been for the last hour, and there was always a certain amount of fear whenever she was left alone. There were so many crazy people in this world, and with a job like hers, she was so vulnerable, yet what else could she do? She and her son needed to eat and jobs were hard to come by.

She mentally crossed herself and muttered a quiet prayer whenever she was alone and a man entered the store. Had Alex noticed her fear, he would have said something to put her at ease, but he didn't notice. He approached the counter and asked for a pack of cigarettes—Lucky Strikes. He wasn't wearing a jacket and his shirt was soaking wet. *He has to be cold*, the clerk thought as she handed him his Luckies. He looked at the pack as if he were confused, then handed it back to her, shaking his head. "Nevermind," he said. Her heart missed a beat. *Was this going to be it?* She looked into his eyes and decided not. She didn't see the hardened face of a criminal, but a friendly, perhaps worried face. Perhaps he was just trying to quit smoking.

"Is there anything else I can get for you?" she asked.

"No. I need some gas, but I'd like to wait for a break in the rain, if you don't mind."

"No problem."

He wandered down by the magazine rack. The clerk tried not to stare at him, but she was still uneasy enough that her eyes kept inadvertently darting his way. She mentally cataloged his appearance as a man in his early forties, slightly bald and a little overweight, maybe thirty or forty pounds more than his frame should be carrying. She memorized the description almost subconsciously, as she did with many of the loiterers at the store, in case she would need to describe him later to the police. Medium height, about five-foot-ten or eleven inches, brown hair, brown eyes, no, they were hazel. His hair was thick on the sides, thin on top, slightly unruly. He was wearing jeans and a pullover knit shirt. She wished she could see the license plate on the red Cherokee, but it was not visible from inside the store.

Alex picked up a magazine, thumbed through it, then picked up another. The thing with the cigarettes really bothered him —Alex didn't smoke! He hadn't touched a cigarette in twenty years, except when playing a role as a CAFI agent.

CAFI is the Combined Armed Forces Intelligence Agency, a super-secret organization that works for the Joint Chiefs of Staff in a role not funded by or visible to Congress. Its existence has passed quite unnoticed from administration to administration because the military leaders have unanimously supported the need for an organization that would meet their security objectives without being under the watchful eye of congressional do-gooders.

Ten years earlier, when he was a CAFI agent, Alex had been an expert at both audio and video subliminal techniques. Now, he was convinced some of those same techniques, perhaps even some newer discoveries, were being used against him. Since CAFI hadn't bothered him during the last ten years, he had decided they were going to leave him alone. Obviously, he had been mistaken.

During those ten years, the Iron Curtain had crumbled, but was now being erected again. With the Soviet Union reassembling itself, and the old school of hardline Communists once again asserting their influence (buoyed as they were by a younger group of Communist radicals who had not yet had their chance at power), relations between the West and the new Soviet block were breaking down. It seemed CAFI wanted Alex Davis again.

The idea CAFI might be trying to draw him into something had begun to haunt Alex the previous morning, when he caught himself thinking in Russian and translating his thoughts into English. He started looking and listening for the source then, but until he saw the radar technology videotape, he had come up with nothing. Since that tape had come from his partner, Alex did not suspect anything until perhaps it was too late.

Ten years was a long time to be away from the espionage game. No one in CAFI had ever assured Alex he wouldn't be called again, but they had left him alone for a long time. He couldn't afford to be pulled back into it. Other things were important to him now. He had done his duty. Now, too much was at stake.

He knew he was rusty, and perhaps that was what bothered him the most. If he started working out to get himself back in shape mentally and physically, he would only be more valuable to them. He was in a dilemma, and he didn't like it. Alex knew he needed to lose some weight, but the excess weight had crept up on him gradually over the past few years, and he had been so tired of having to stay in shape all the time he just let it happen. Now any attempt to take the weight off was more of a struggle than he had time for. His dark brown hair was beginning to show signs of gray. He was forty-two years old. Some days he felt fifty.

The rain let up and Alex pumped his gas. Instead of going home, he drove to Addison Airport, to the hangar where the company's airplane was kept—a Cessna 182. The cold front had passed through, bringing behind it clear skies and strong winds. Alex took off in the Cessna and spent the last hour of daylight flying around the outskirts of the Metroplex trying to formulate a plan. He knew he had to confront CAFI, but how would he do it? Earlier, he had tried phoning J. L. McDaniels, CAFI's director, but either the telephone switching system used by agents to contact headquarters had been changed, or Alex's code had been deleted from the system. He couldn't imagine the system changing—it hadn't been altered during the ten years he had used it, but the fact his code may have been removed was a good sign. He could go to San Antonio in person, confront McDaniels, and tell him he wanted no part of whatever it was CAFI was scheming. He had to do something quickly or it would be too late. CAFI only bet on a sure thing, and they hedged their bets a long time before the race. Using subliminal techniques was part of the process and they were very good at it.

As the rain showers moved out of the Metroplex, the city was left with a clean, fresh look, as if it had just been washed. Here and there water flowed rapidly through streams and ditches, while the various forks of the Trinity River were swollen from the runoff. Off to the west, the sun appeared briefly beneath a layer of clouds and bathed the wet earth in yellow light just before making its way into the haze layer where it would turn blood red during its descent. This was Alex's favorite time of day to be flying, but the cold front had brought with it strong, low-level winds that made the ride too bumpy to really enjoy. He headed back to the airport, his emotions as unsettled as the turbulence buffeting the small plane.

When Alex landed at Addison Airport, he was still undecided about what to do. He would feel pretty foolish confronting McDaniels if CAFI wasn't wanting him after all—if the whole thing was just his imagination. Why give McDaniels a shot at him if he wasn't sure?

That night at home, Alex sat with his family. He wouldn't watch TV. He tried to listen as Susan began telling him about her activities that afternoon, and about things the kids had done or said, but his mind kept wandering. Susan was bothered by Alex's distraction, but not worried. She had seen her husband preoccupied many times. That was just Alex. When he had something on his mind, you might as well be talking to a brick wall. Usually it was because some business matter was pressing him. Sometimes he shared his thoughts with her, sometimes he didn't. Susan tried not to pry, but she really cared about the things Alex was involved in and it hurt her not to be included.

Around eight o'clock, Alex announced he was going to the library.

"Good," Susan responded, "I'll send the kids to bed and get Jeannine to come over and stay with them until we get back."

"Not tonight, hon," Alex replied. "There's some research I need to do. It won't take long."

Susan was disappointed. During the early years of their marriage, they'd enjoyed many hours together at the library looking up topics of interest or answers to questions they'd asked each other.

Alex pretended not to notice Susan's disappointment. He leaned over, kissed her on the cheek, and went to get his coat. A minute later, Susan heard him drive off. She sat willed herself not to be hurt by Alex's shutting her out. "Dear Lord," she muttered a silent prayer, "whatever is bothering him, let me help if I can."

Alex fully intended to drive straight to the SMU library. He wanted to look up everything he could find on subliminal communications. There was a very good possibility new discoveries had been made since he had been actively involved with the techniques. But, as he drove by a neighborhood clinic, his thoughts turned to Karen Webster. He stopped at a pay phone and called her.

Karen was Alex's doctor, his adopted sister and one of his best friends. When Alex was nine, his parents and younger brother had perished in a tragic house fire. He'd been away at a Cub Scout meeting when it happened. When neither of his parents showed up to pick him up after the meeting, one of the Den Mothers drove Alex home. It wasn't a short drive, for the Davises lived several miles outside of town on a 200-acre farm on which Alex's father barely eked out a living.

As the Den Mother's station wagon turned down the narrow gravel road toward the Davis farm, they came upon a scene that would be forever etched in Alex's mind.

The driveway was lined with emergency vehicles with flashing lights. Ambulances, police cars, fire engines—it seemed the whole county was there. Beyond the lights were the smoldering ruins of what had been the Davis home.

The Den Mother stopped at the end of the driveway and Alex got out of the car, his eyes wide with disbelief, his heart pounding in his chest. He walked up the driveway in a daze, hardly comprehending what he was seeing. He searched for his family among the workers who quietly went about the business of rolling up fire hoses, stringing up yellow tape and stowing their equipment. He expected to find his parents in the yard, near the car or standing with a group of neighbors.

Eagerly, he searched for the familiar face of his mother, who would tell him everything would be all right, or his father, who would be helping the workers. His mother would put her arm around his shoulders, squeeze him to her and say, "It's all right, Alex. We've been through tough times before." But neither parent was to be found. Maybe they'd gone to town to get him after all.

When he saw the car in the driveway, panic set in. Alex ran toward the house. A woman broke from the pack and grabbed him as he ran by. Holding his arm, she pulled him toward her. He looked into her face, hoping it was his mother, but the face was that of Stella Webster, one of their nearest neighbors and his mother's best friend. Stella had a strange look in her eyes as she pulled Alex to her, a look of fear and sympathy and horror all rolled into one. A girl, about his age, wrapped her arms around him in a bear hug. It was Karen—a classmate, a playmate, Stella's daughter and Alex's friend.

"It's going to be all right, Alex," the girl said. "You can come and live with us."

He looked at her, fear and shock in his eyes. She must have thought at that moment Alex had gone berserk and surely she must let him go for fear of being struck, but still she held on. Alex strained to look over his shoulder. There was activity going on at the house.

"No, don't look!" Karen exclaimed.

He tried to pull away from her, but stopped dead in his tracks. Workers were coming out of the ruins bearing three stretchers. Upon each was a blanket-covered lump. Alex took all of this in as if in slow motion. He knew what the lumps were, but they were smaller than they should have been, the last the smallest of all, as if almost nothing. To Alex it felt like a giant hand reached into his chest, grabbed his heart and squeezed until he thought it would burst. "No, no!" he sobbed, sinking to his knees. Karen knelt with him, never letting him go, her little arms holding him solidly around the shoulders.

For a few months after that, Alex went to live with his father's sister. But the woman had no understanding of the needs of a young boy, and no real way to provide for him. Her home in town was too small and too confining for the boy. Within six months, he was living with the Websters. Before the year was out, they filed the papers necessary to adopt him.

Karen was the youngest child in their rather large family. She was nine, the same age as Alex, and because her real brothers and sisters were several years older, the two youngsters enjoyed an especially close relationship. Perhaps it was the fact they were not blood relatives that caused them not to have the usual friction typical of brothers and sisters. They played together as youngsters, and throughout their teenage years, each found in the other an understanding friend and confidant. Their relationship passed through many stages, including some brief romantic interludes, but for the most part, they were just good friends.

Shortly after high school graduation, Alex was drafted into the Army. After Basic Training, he was sent to Texas to learn to fly helicopters. While he was away, Karen entered the University to study pre-med. By the time Alex returned from his first tour in Vietnam, Karen was well on her way to medical school. Now she had a thriving practice in North Dallas.

From the earliest days, Karen became so involved in her work she had little time for romance. She was everybody's friend and nobody's girlfriend. The result was she had never married. Because Karen didn't have a husband, and because Alex was raised in the tradition a woman needed a man to watch out for her, he felt a sense of responsibility for her, such as a brother might feel for an unmarried sister. Sometimes weeks, even months, passed with little contact between them. Yet whenever they were together, it was always as if no time had passed since their last meeting. Theirs was a friendship tested and proven by time and circumstances, and which miles and years never seemed to affect.

As he made the call, Alex chided himself for the fact that too often he depended upon Susan to keep in touch with Karen. Now he was calling her because he wanted something. He felt the need to talk to Karen about what he was feeling because Karen knew about his days with CAFI and Susan did not.

They arranged to meet for lunch the next day. Karen had surgery scheduled for both the morning and the afternoon, so he would have to meet her at a restaurant near the hospital.

After the phone call, Alex's spirits were lifted. Karen was an eternal optimist, always enthusiastic, always seeing the bright side of everything. She just might have some input into how Alex could solve his problem with CAFI and their efforts to compel him back into service through the use of their subliminal techniques.

At the library, Alex became engrossed in what he could find on the subject of subliminal communication. Though he was familiar with most of the concepts, there was now more to guard against than he had imagined. The body of research available (and not withheld from the public in the name of national security) had increased dramatically in the years since Alex had reviewed the literature. The use of videotape as opposed to film, provided a more suitable medium and one which could more easily be manipulated. Video was much more effective primarily because of its speed and the availability of electronic editing equipment and techniques. In the early days, when film had been the prominent medium, the effectiveness of subliminal messages was limited to the use of some type of audio or combination audio and visual rhythm to first hypnotize the intended victim to a degree. This was followed by a message hidden within the twenty-four, single-field frames per second on the film. The effectiveness of most of these techniques was limited. Certainly, the success rate was much lower than with video.

With videotape, there are thirty frames per second to work with, and within each frame there are two fields. That medium makes it rather simple to imbed visual symbols in a hypnotic pattern and then follow them up with visual messages that pass by the eye too fast to be recognized, but which transfer information to the subconscious.

Alex was looking for something different, something new. He had only watched one video in recent months, but still CAFI was getting to him. They must be using some new technique to supplement the limited video exposure, yet he couldn't find a clue in any of the books that gave him an indication of what he should be avoiding. He left the library with his senses sharpened, but with no real answers.

2

Alex recognized Karen's Silver Mercedes as he turned into the parking lot of Ninfa's Mexican Restaurant. The "Lady Doc" personalized license plates were a dead giveaway. The plates fit. In most people's eyes, Karen Webster was every bit a lady and every bit a doctor. He looked at his watch, hoping he had not kept her waiting. *Good*, he thought, *she's early*.

Inside the restaurant, Alex quickly located Karen seated at a booth along the back wall. The setup was perfect. Hers was the only occupied booth in the small area leading to the patio. There was a fountain in the center with water cascading down from a beautiful bronze basin into an octagonal-shaped pool below. He and Karen would be able to talk and the sound of the water would prevent anyone from hearing their "sensitive" conversation. She was facing the entrance and saw Alex come in. She waved him over. Chips, hot sauce and iced tea were already on the table.

Karen probed Alex's eyes as he sat down. She read him like a book. "What's wrong, Alex?" she asked.

"Either I'm losing my mind or the agency wants me again." Alex's relationship with the super-secret organization had been, and still was, highly classified. Karen knew about it because she had participated in his recruitment. She was never part of CAFI, but had played a unique role in the development of one of its most successful deep-Soviet penetrators—Alex Davis.

"Some medium—I don't know what it is yet—is being used to prepare me for a CAFI assignment."

"You're kidding me! What makes you think they want you now?" It wasn't meant as a put-down question, but a simple question of amazement.

Alex took his napkin off the table and spread it across his lap. He wasn't put off by the question, but he had a point to make. "You should know as well as anybody. The hardliners are back in power. The Soviet Union is emerging again as a Communist/Socialist state. They give the appearance of being open, but they are only open to take. There is no give in their agenda."

"I'm not sure it's as bad as you're picturing it," Karen said, "but I will admit many of the old Communist leaders have regained some semblance of power."

"You see it through rose-colored glasses," Alex told her. He knew Karen had a soft spot in her heart for Russia because of recent trips she had made there as part of some kind of missions program.

"So you think CAFI wants you back as a spy so you can keep an eye on things over there?"

"Could be," Alex answered, missing her tongue-in-cheek humor entirely. "I can't find the source of their contact, so I haven't been able to break it." He looked across the room, then turned back toward her, trying to sound convincing. "Whatever it is they want me to do, I don't want any part of it." He hesitated. "At least I don't think I do. But I must have some kind of open door they're exploiting, or they couldn't affect me like they are."

Karen leaned across the table toward Alex, showing sincere interest. "Just for the sake of argument, what do you think they want you to do?"

"I don't know the details, but I think it involves flying. I think they want me to discover the mission myself and then want to do it."

"Why?"

"That's a safe approach for them. That way they won't have to admit any knowledge of what I'm doing if it turns out the mission isn't successful. If I initiate the mission on my own, they can keep their hands clean."

"I don't understand."

"It's just the way they work," Alex explained. "I've used the same general techniques myself. What puzzles me is I'm no novice. They shouldn't be able to get to me without my knowing how."

"Perhaps it's a new technique, something they've developed since you left the organization."

"I've thought of that. In fact, I've done some reading on the subject, but I haven't figured it out." He looked thoughtful. Karen smiled as she recognized the wheels turning in his brain. "It's got to be something I'm not famliar with," he said. "And it bothers me that it's something I don't know how to guard against."

"Are you sure you want to?" It was a typical Karen question. She wasted no time in probing to the depths of whatever a person was thinking.

"Why would you say that?" Alex asked. "You know I walked away from all of that when I married Susan. I have a family, a business … responsibilities." He patted his stomach. "I'm out of shape. I haven't spoken Russian in years. I don't fly anything bigger or faster than a single-engine Cessna. Why would I want to expose myself to the danger and uncertainty of espionage again?"

"Because you believe in what they're doing," she told him.

They were interrupted by the waitress who took their order. When the waitress left, Karen reached across the table and touched Alex's arm. "Alex," she said, "If they want you, it's because they know you're the best man for the job. And if they're really wanting you to come back after all of these years, they must feel like they don't have anyone else they can trust to do it. You should at least find out what it is."

Alex shook his head. "It doesn't work that way, Karen. If I know what it is, I'm already committed. They control their information so tightly, even the agents being used for the contact don't know what's happening. If it was something as simple as a 'yes' or 'no' decision, McDaniels would just call me up, set up a lunch appointment, and tell me what he wanted. If he was that sure of his mission, and sure I would accept, that's all he would have to do. But it's not working that way."

Alex was getting worked up, as if trying to convince himself as well as Karen. He continued, "He knows I would say 'no' to almost anything he asked, unless I truly believed I really was the only one who could do it and it had to be done."

"Why does he know that?"

"Because I told him I wanted out when Susan and I got married. He agreed, if I would finish the assignment I was on, which I did."

"Now you think he's suddenly decided to call you back into the game?"

"It looks like it. Obviously, something is going on related to the new Soviet Union."

"And so he's using some kind of subliminal techniques to get the message to you, rather than just a direct contact?"

Alex nodded. "First, he's got to prepare me, to give me bits and pieces of the picture until I begin to formulate the plan in my own mind. Then, he has to send messages and people my way that appear to be unrelated, but who fill in the gaps in my information. These people won't even know they are being used. It's a fine art, Karen, and they are good at it. Evidently, they are even better than when I played the game. The thing is, I want to be able to make my decision before I'm in too deep. And unless I'm sadly mistaken, I want my decision to be 'no, I don't want to do it.'"

Sensing Alex's agitation, Karen attempted to change the subject. "By the way, I'm going to Moscow in a few weeks to the International Conference on Internal Medicine."

"Really?" Alex retorted. "Well that's great timing."

This announcement only served to reinforce the thought that had been nagging at him for the past several minutes—Karen could be a part of this whole thing, either knowingly or unwittingly. He looked at her intently. "Are you part of this? Are you and McDaniels up to something?"

"Don't be silly. I haven't seen Mac in years."

"You're sure about that?" He tried to read her eyes. She had always been able to see through him. He wished he could say the same about his ability to read her. In some ways, she was like all other women—a total mystery to the men who are close to them.

She rolled her eyes. "No, Alex," she assured him. "I'm not part of some diabolical plot on the part of CAFI to turn you into a spy again. Besides, the organization might have been disbanded by now. It's possible with all the changes in administration and the trend toward openness, that the military commanders were no longer able to keep CAFI a secret from Congress."

"It's possible, but not really likely. They guarded CAFI's secret closely. With the emasculation of the CIA and the breakdowns in the National Security Agency, an organization like CAFI is more important now than ever."

"Whether they're still around or not, I don't have anything to do with them," Karen declared. "My reason for going to Moscow is simple. I've been selected by the American Medical Association as a delegate to an international conference on surgical procedures because of some of the work I've been doing in the field of micro-laser surgery."

"How many times have you been to Russia?" Alex asked.

"This will be my fourth trip, but it's the first time I've been in any kind of official capacity. It's really an honor to have been selected."

"It is," he affirmed, patting her on the arm and smiling. "I'm proud of you. When are you going?"

"In three weeks."

"That's kind of sudden, isn't it?"

"Actually, it's been a little touch and go about whether or not I was going to go. I had to have my visa renewed, and the fact I've been in the country several times before, is apparently a problem."

"What do you mean?" Alex asked.

"I guess they are changing the rules a bit," Karen admitted. "But this conference is so visible they wouldn't dare raise a stink by denying the American representative a visa."

"The American representative? As in the only one?" That sounded pretty far-fetched to Alex. In spite of all the hoopla about Healthcare reform and Managed Care programs that were following in the footsteps of Canada's socialized system, the United States was still the leader in medical technology. At least Alex thought it was.

"That's right," Karen answered. "So it really is quite an honor to have been chosen."

"No underlying agendas or motives?"

"None that I know of."

"Well, I'm happy for you," Alex said, and he was. Alex had always been somewhat amazed at Karen's accomplishments. She was a backwoods country girl from Tennessee who had become an internationally recognized surgeon.

Karen began to share with Alex about what she hoped to accomplish on the trip. Watching her face and the intensity with which she approached the subject of international medicine, Alex's respect for her work increased, yet it still dimmed alongside his respect for her as a person.

Karen's skin was smooth and wrinkle free, except for the laugh lines in the corners of her eyes. Her lips were full, her teeth white and straight. Altogether, it was a mouth designed to smile. When she listened to you, her gray-blue eyes radiated warmth and seemed to penetrate into your heart. She hung onto every word, nodding understanding, as if there was nothing on earth more important than what you were telling her right then and there. She asked penetrating questions that let you know she was listening and what you were saying was important. When she was talking, her eyes danced with enthusiasm, taking her listeners in, making them believe what she was telling you was of the utmost importance and encouraging agreement.

Karen had really kept herself well. She exercised regularly and jogged almost daily. Her hair was full and short and beginning to show signs of gray, which helped her peers look beyond her attractiveness as a woman and respect her professional abilities.

None of her physical attributes mattered to Alex—he'd been around her all his life. What he saw was a person who had an inner quality that went beyond his understanding, but which made people glad they knew her. The fact is, Karen knew something about life Alex had not grasped.

It hadn't always been that way. True, she had always cared about people. True, she had always been a giver. And, even as a little girl, Karen had seemed mature beyond her years. But something happened to her while Alex was in Vietnam; something that brought about a radical change in her life. Alex noticed she was different when he returned home during leave and asked her about it. She went to great length to explain to him how she had experienced an encounter with God. This encounter had resulted in something she called being "born again."

Karen wanted Alex to share in the experience, too, but there was something about it Alex just did not understand. The Websters had always been a religious family. Alex had attended church with them, and shared the same beliefs they did. Karen tried to tell him this was something different—something more real and tangible—but somehow she was never able to explain it to Alex's satisfaction. He believed what she told him, and was happy for her, but it all seemed so mystical to him, so unlike her, he was not able to appropriate any meaning in it for himself. Whatever it was, it was still with her more than twenty years later, and it made her more beautiful than ever.

While Karen had never been able to communicate this "born again" experience to Alex successfully, it had made sense to Susan. She had jumped right on it, and she claimed she was born again too. Karen and Susan shared a lot Alex didn't understand. Sometimes he felt like they were ganging up on him to make sure he lived right and went to heaven. He was doing all right, he thought. No major sins, and he did believe in God. He figured he'd do all right when it came to convincing St. Peter to let him in.

As Karen talked about her upcoming trip, Alex tried to listen, but much of what she was telling him simply went right over his head. Karen suddenly realized she had swung the conversation off Alex's problem and onto herself. She had gotten wrapped up in telling him about her trip. He was being polite, but he wasn't really listening. She had been rambling on about her life and her work and it was Alex who had called *her* because he needed to talk out this perceived problem going on in his life. She mentally chided herself for being so selfish. Suddenly, she had a thought. "Alex, I'm not sure why I feel this way, but I think you should go for it."

"Go for it?"

"Think about it. You need a change. Susan was telling me the other day you seem to be bored, you've lost some of your drive and some of your ambition. Maybe this mission with CAFI, if that's what it is, will give you a chance to prove to yourself you really still have what it takes, that you can take on a challenge and overcome it."

"Come on, Karen. I'm too old for that kind of stuff."

"Right, old man," she answered. "You're forty-two. So am I and I'm just getting started."

After lunch, Alex went back to his office and called Susan.

"Hi, hon. What are you doing?"

"What do you mean, 'what am I doing?' I'm just sitting around watching soap operas."

He knew she was kidding. Susan hated soap operas. In fact, she hated most of what was on TV. "If I were to break away and come home, will you be there?"

"Of course I will," she told him. "I've hardly seen you for the past few days. We need to spend some time together."

"Great. I feel that way, too. I'll see you in a little bit."

Susan called one of the neighbors and asked her to pick up the kids from school and keep them a while. When Alex came home they had the place to themselves and took full advantage of the privacy.

Later that afternoon, they were in the kitchen putting a snack together. Alex was standing at the counter slicing some cheese when Susan broached the subject of the library.

"What was it you were looking for at the library last night?"

"It was some research about something I used to know a lot about, but have lost touch with." The way he answered the question was meant to leave the impression it was work related. He didn't want to lie to her and technically, he figured he hadn't. But he couldn't tell her about CAFI. It was for her own protection, as much as anything. He hoped she wouldn't press him for more details, and was relieved when she didn't.

They sat at the table, munching on cheese and crackers. Susan was aware Alex was not being entirely truthful with her. She wanted to trust him, but sometimes it was hard. Often he lived in a world of his own, and it seemed to her as if he could go right on living without her and the kids and it wouldn't make any difference to him at all. It was as if he went through all the motions of being a husband and father because he knew what those motions were supposed to be, but not because his

David B. Freeman

full heart was in it. This particular afternoon he had come home to be with her because he thought that was what was needed to clear the air between them, but it wasn't. He let the wall down just a little bit, went through the motions of being a husband and a lover, but the wall was still there."

It was his trip to the library the night before that aroused her doubts. He hadn't been to the library without her in a long time. When he said he was going, she thought it was quite unusual he didn't want to include her. A babysitter for the kids was a phone call away.

Researching subjects together had been an unofficial hobby of theirs over the years. Whenever someone asked a question neither of them knew how to answer, they would go to the library and look it up. They called it "expanding their horizons." Both had learned a lot that way. Susan had an inquisitive mind and was always eager to learn something new. She loved it when Alex included her in his business dealings because it indicated his trust in her and his appreciation for her mental faculties. Too, the library held a special meaning for them because they had met at the library at Memphis State University.

Alex had been stationed at Millington Naval Air Station north of Memphis, where he was assigned as an Instructor Pilot in the primary jet training school. His military assignment had been a cover. Four deep plant Soviet agents were in training as Navy pilots, and their cover had been exceptional. Alex's assignment was to verify their identities, discover their contacts and their purpose, and to insure the Navy could control any information to which the Soviets might gain access.

It was believed the KGB intended to get at least one of the students into the Navy Test Pilot School where they would have access to the latest Navy aircraft. Since Alex was a graduate of that school, he had special insight into the path the students would have to take. It was his job to make sure the right one made it. CAFI had plans for that young Soviet agent. Alex could only guess what they would be.

While stationed at Millington, Alex started working on his Master's Degree. He attended classes at Memphis State several nights a week. When he met Susan, for the first time in his career, he began having trouble keeping his mind on his job. She was a small girl, yet well proportioned. Alex's first attraction to her had admittedly been physical. With her full head of bouncing blonde curls, her light green eyes, and her infectious laugh, Susan had affected Alex in a way no other woman had.

He kept finding excuses to go to the campus, hoping he might see her. He often found her in the library and finally succeeded in getting her to go out with him. The fact he was a pilot did not impress her. In fact, nothing about him seemed to impress her. Alex found himself at a total loss in trying to find a way to get Susan to show more than a casual interest in him. Yet the more he was around her, the more attracted to her he became. Besides her good looks, he found she had a sharp wit and was well versed on many subjects.

Susan had come to Memphis State on a music scholarship, yet after she was there, she changed her major to special education. Her goal was to work with and teach handicapped or retarded children. As Alex had grown to know her, he found Susan was a woman filled with compassion. Her whole life seemed to be consumed with the desire to help those who were less fortunate. Even though she had continued to go out with him, Alex was frustrated by the fact she wouldn't let him get too close to her. It seemed to him she got close to everybody else. Finally, Alex told Susan the Navy was transferring him. Actually, he was going to Langley Field in Virginia for a couple of months, and after that he would be back at Millington. But he didn't tell Susan he would be back. Alex had made the decision he would do well to try to forget her since she apparently had no more than a casual interest in him.

The next time he saw her, it was at the Naval Air Base the day he returned from Langley. After reporting in, Alex drove to the house he had rented on the base. Susan arrived there fifteen minutes later. She knew all along he was coming back. She wanted to give the relationship time so she could find out in her own way if it was real. She had to know for sure that he was the one for her and that day she knew. They were married a month later.

Three months after the wedding, Alex flew a Navy jet to San Antonio to see J. L. McDaniels, CAFI's director. Alex told the director he wanted out now that he was married. J. L. reminded him of his contract. It was for life if the agency needed him. Under certain conditions, he could be called back at any time. Alex knew he had agreed to such conditions, but he tried to convince J. L. keeping him active would be against CAFI's best interest. He had served them well—now he needed some time to develop his own life. J. L. promised to let him go, but not until he finished his present assignment. He would see the young Soviets through training and insure the one they wanted to go to the Test Pilot School would be the one to make the grades.

After the Navy assignment, Alex went into business with two of his former classmates from Memphis State. They formed a company called DEW, Inc., named for the three founders: Alex Davis, Bud Ewing and Ken Webb. They pronounced the name of the company "Doing," the way Dew, Inc. sounded when spoken with their southern accents. DEW, Inc. began supplying electronic measuring devices and communications equipment to the military. The business did quite well for the three partners. When the operation expanded, Alex and Bud moved to Dallas and opened up offices and manufacturing facilities at Addison Airport. Ken Webb continued to run the Memphis branch.

J. L. convinced Alex not to tell Susan about his years with CAFI. He explained to Alex the knowledge might endanger her life some day. Karen Webster was a different story. She knew something about CAFI, though maybe not about Alex's assignments within the organization. Karen had helped convince Alex joining CAFI was the right thing to do.

So Alex had kept that part of his past a secret from Susan, which was easy enough to do, because there had always been an alternate life for Alex Davis when on a CAFI assignment. As far as Susan knew, Alex had joined the Army when he was nineteen and had later transferred to the Navy. He had been on active duty for twelve years and had been a pilot most of those years. She believed he served three tours in Vietnam, one while in the Army and two while in the Navy. Susan had no way of knowing what the real nature of those tours had been. In actuality, Alex had spent most of those years in the Soviet Union under cover. He had been instrumental in helping the United States gather firsthand information about Soviet technology in the area of jet fighters, weapon and navigation systems. He had been so successfully implanted into the Soviet military structure, he had flown Soviet jets and helicopters on many training missions and on real missions in Afghanistan.

Here they sat in their kitchen, ten years later, with Alex stubbornly holding onto a secret that possibly no longer mattered, but just as possibly mattered a great deal, and Susan feeling hurt because her husband wouldn't tell her about something apparently very important to him. Husbands and wives weren't supposed to have secrets.

3

Karen Webster left for Moscow on a Saturday morning in late March. Alex and Susan drove her to the airport. Karen talked excitedly to Susan about the trip while Alex, at the wheel of Karen's Mercedes, was absorbed in his own thoughts.

Karen, who was riding in the front passenger seat and talking to Susan over her shoulder, noticed Alex was in his own world and tried to bring him out of it. "What's the matter, brother? Aren't you the least bit excited your sister is representing the surgical community of the whole USA at a big worldwide medical conference?"

"Huh?" Alex turned to look at her. "I'm sorry, Karen, it's just there is something going on with the business that has me a little distracted."

"Okay," Karen replied. "You're forgiven. But give it a rest. You've got your business all the time. You don't get that many chances to spend time with me."

"That's true, Alex," Susan chided from the back seat. "You've hardly shown any interest at all in Karen's trip and it means so much to her."

"I'm sorry," Alex replied.

It was true Alex's thoughts were not on Karen's trip. He was thinking about a conversation with Bud Ewing that had occurred the night before. Bud wanted DEW, Inc. to buy an airplane—not just any airplane, but one of nine Windecker Eagles that had been built. Of the original nine airplanes, at least three of them had been damaged, destroyed or dismantled. One of the planes had been donated to the Smithsonian Institute. The Air Force owned one which was now in the Army Aviation Museum at Fort Rucker. Of the ones still flying, Leo Windecker, the plane's designer had serial #4.

A businessman who lived in Ohio had just purchased the manufacturing rights to the Eagle and owned three of the planes. One of the three was now for sale. Bud thought the plane had potential for two reasons: one was as an investment; the other, a more practical reason—the Windecker Eagle was the forerunner of stealth technology. An all-composite airplane, it was virtually invisible to radar. It had not been designed for that purpose, but that characteristic had been an interesting phenomenon which had opened the doors to the stealth bomber and F-117 development. Bud saw potential for DEW, Inc. to use the Eagle as a test bed for a new discreet radar signal scrambler device the company was developing for the military. The composite, radar-invisible plane would have distinct advantages in testing such a device. Alex thought it an unusual approach and was not at all sure Bud knew what he was doing. Still, the thought of owning one of the few remaining Windecker Eagles definitely appealed to the pilot in Alex. He had always been fascinated with the Eagle and the man who had designed it. But now he put the thoughts of the Eagle aside and turned his attention toward the two women in his life.

After Karen's plane departed DFW, Alex and Susan stopped at a restaurant near the airport for something to eat. They'd no sooner sat down at a table when Susan asked, "What's got you so preoccupied this morning, Alex? Is it the plane Bud talked to you about last night?"

"Yes. The project Bud is working on is a long shot, and I don't know if we can invest the money right now for a plane for just that project."

"But you want to, right?"

"I've always been fascinated by the Windecker. The truth is, I just want to own it whether it makes sense or not. That's not like me, is it?"

Susan laughed. "No, it's not. But you haven't really been your normal self lately, have you?"

"I guess not," Alex replied, taking her arm in his and patting her hand. "Thanks for putting up with me."

"Oh, you just think I'm putting up with you," Susan joked. "I'll find a way to make you pay!"

They laughed and joked throughout the meal. Alex seemed more like his old self. As soon as they got home, he called Bud. "Let's buy the plane, Bud. How soon can we pick it up?"

On Monday morning Bud made the necessary calls. That afternoon he and Alex flew to Phoenix to see the plane. The Eagle was in a hangar at the Sun City Airport. It had not been flown for several years. Alex examined the airframe and engine logbooks to determine what was necessary to put the airplane back in an airworthy condition. The plane was apparently sound mechanically, but needed some FAA inspections before it would be legal to fly. The engine would also need to be disassembled and inspected for rust or metal fatigue after sitting for so long.

After looking over the plane, the two men went into the office of George Wilkes, the owner's representative.

"Why is this airplane for sale?" Alex wanted to know.

"There have been some difficulties in getting the aircraft back into production," Wilkes explained. "The project has been abandoned, at least by the original investors. They think this airplane is now valuable only as a collector's item." Bud Ewing had other ideas, but he kept quiet. Alex negotiated the details of the transaction and they settled on $150,000. The buyer was responsible for making the plane airworthy.

The two men boarded their plane to return to Dallas after making arrangements for all the necessary inspections to be completed. Alex was to return to Phoenix in two weeks to fly the Eagle to Dallas.

During the airline flight, Bud brought Alex up to date on the transponder project. "The transponder is designed to multiply and displace radar returns for military purposes."

"I understand that," Alex said. "But how does it work?"

"Let me get into that in a minute," Bud replied. "But first, I want you to fully understand why it is I felt we needed an airplane like the Eagle."

"I'm listening."

"The desired effect is to make one aircraft appear as if it is multiple planes. An additional benefit of the technology is you can electronically displace a single aircraft from its actual location, as far as radar is concerned."

"You mean the signal that the ground-based radar unit receives from the aircraft's transponder appears to be coming from some location other than where it actually is?"

"You got it."

"Why?"

"Think about it," Bud answered excitedly. "The purpose of the original design criteria should be obvious—to make one aircraft appear as if it were many."

Alex nodded.

"The second benefit is a byproduct of the first. In order to make one aircraft appear in multiple locations, you have to be able to project the radar signal some distance from where the airplane actually is, right?"

"True," Alex agreed.

"Well, there you have it. We can let the transponder—actually, I'm going to call it a 'disponder'—randomly select the range and azimuth of the false signals, or we can give that ability to the pilot. We did both. The single displacement feature occurs when we select one false target and then mask the original signal."

"Okay, I've got it," Alex said. "By the way, I like that name—disponder. I assume it stands for 'displaced transponder'."

"Right. Now back to the Eagle. Because of its composite construction, the Windecker Eagle is virtually invisible as a primary radar target. It will make an ideal test bed for the initial testing of the scrambling transponder."

"But there are a whole lot of homebuilts with composite construction," Alex interjected.

"That's true," Bud replied. "But none as stable a platform and with the weight-carrying capability of the Windecker."

"Okay, I'll buy that. What's the testing plan?"

Bud was enjoying Alex's interest in his project. Though it was already sold to the military as a concept, getting a production contract was a different story. That was Alex's strongest contribution to the company. Bud and Ken took care of the technical details; Alex was best at handling the business end of the venture.

"The testing will have to be done very discreetly," Bud answered. "We will have to conduct it in military airspace for safety and security reasons."

"Question," Alex interrupted. "Is it all right if we use the Eagle for company transportation?" Alex was looking forward to exploring the Eagle's flight characteristics. Having had the privilege of flying many different types of aircraft, both Soviet and American, Alex still enjoyed the challenge of getting acquainted with a new type. That was one of the things which had made him so valuable in his days with CAFI.

"I guess so, except when the testing program is going full swing," Bud answered. "By the way, you'll have to make the test flights. This thing is too classified for us to bring in a contract pilot and I can't fly the tests and monitor the results at the same time."

"No problem," Alex assured him. Bud was a pilot, but he wasn't a commercial pilot and he had no military experience.

During the last hour of the flight, Bud became engrossed in a magazine. Alex leaned back in his seat, closed his eyes, and let his mind wander back to his days with CAFI.

Alex was recruited by CAFI during his final weeks of Army helicopter training. All of the flight training candidates were subjected to a battery of tests which they were told would help the Army determine their career paths. Alex's test results were especially interesting to the intelligence analysts. CAFI needed an individual with Alex's particular aptitudes and abilities, but they also needed a man with certain personality traits. These were traits Alex Davis apparently had, at least according to the preliminary testing. He was interviewed by the CAFI recruiters without him knowing who they were, or who they represented. On his third interview, he met J. L. McDaniels, the director of CAFI.

J. L. told Alex about the organization, an organization about which very little is known. McDaniels explained to Alex that CAFI consisted of a small group of select men and women who worked in support of the other intelligence agencies, both military and civilian. Army Intelligence, Navy Intelligence, Air Force Intelligence, the CIA and the National Security Agency all depended upon CAFI's agents for certain types of highly specialized and sensitive intelligence gathering missions. CAFI agents had no official identity. They all had normal military jobs and worked entirely undercover when on an intelligence assignment. The recruiting promises were intriguing to Alex. He would see the world. He would receive a lot of highly specialized and demanding training.

On most of his assignments he would be working alone. The missions would be dangerous. Because of the amount and type of training he would receive, he would be required to agree to allow the government to press him into service any time it was necessary for reasons of national security. For all of this, he would be paid his standard military pay. Any more than that could possibly call special attention to him.

The training would be invaluable. That and the chance to serve his country in a way that was offered to few others, CAFI felt was remuneration enough. J. L. was certain Alex would take the job; otherwise they would have never met face to face. Nevertheless, he had taken certain precautions in the way of enlisting the aide of one Karen Webster.

Karen's roommate in college was Judy McDaniels, J. L.'s daughter, who was also studying to be a doctor. On weekends, Karen Webster often visited the McDaniels' home in San Antonio. During their junior year, Judy McDaniels was diagnosed with stomach cancer. The cancer took her fast, but not without a lot of pain and suffering. Karen Webster stood by her friend to the end, even to the point of missing an entire semester of college studies. She practically became a member of the McDaniels family, and J. L. was especially fond of her.

A few months after Judy's death, Karen was in San Antonio and stopped by McDaniels' office for a visit. Quite by accident, she noticed a folder on his desk with the name Alex Davis on it. "That's funny," she commented, "my adopted brother's name is Alex Davis."

"I know," McDaniels answered. "It's the same guy. Karen, I need your help …."

Alex joined CAFI immediately upon completing flight training. He then spent a year in Vietnam as a combat helicopter pilot. He also spent that year, and parts of several years thereafter, learning the Russian language.

Russian is not an easy language to learn, but Alex had a head start. A friend of his in high school had descended from Russian immigrants. His friend's grandfather was a gunsmith with a shop on the outskirts of the small town in Tennessee where Alex and Karen grew up. Fascinated with the man's handiwork, Alex asked if he could work for him in the afternoons after school. Russian was the man's native language. He was still struggling to learn English. Alex helped whenever he could, and in turn he picked up quite a bit of Russian. CAFI's methods added to what Alex already knew. They had some very effective teaching aids, including the use of video and audio tapes which used subliminal techniques to teach the accent, the body language, the colloquialisms and the mannerisms that would make Alex's command of the language complete and authentic.

Alex learned Russian during his waking hours, and he learned it at night, in his sleep. He doubted some of CAFI's methods when he was first told about them, but they had worked. By the end of the first year, he could read and speak Russian as if it were his native language. In subsequent years, he became even more polished, finally learning to even think in Russian instead of having to translate.

Upon returning from his first tour in Vietnam, Alex was told to apply himself toward being accepted as one of nine Army officers who were being allowed to attend the Navy's Test Pilot school that year. Alex was accepted (he never knew for sure if he had done it on his own, or if CAFI had fixed it for him) and graduated the course with top honors. Within a year, he made an inter-service transfer and became a Navy officer. He worked as a Navy Test Pilot during the day, but spent his evenings and weekends in special classes CAFI set up for him. Already a natural actor, Alex became an expert at voice impersonations and at disguises. He was taught Soviet habits and customs and constantly worked on his mastery of the language. His first real assignment sent him to Russia, where he replaced a Soviet Air Force Major.

Major Grigori Kotosvk was a pilot in the Soviet Air Force. He was also a CIA operative. Major Kotosvk had served as a vital link in the CIA's pipeline into the Soviet Air Force since his recruitment in the early sixties. His former commander had defected to the United States and was instrumental in helping the CIA contact Kotosvk. One of the things that made CAFI want Alex was his resemblance to Grigori Kotosvk. The two men were almost identical in physical appearance.

One of the major problems the CIA had with the Kotosvk link was the Soviet's inability to get detailed information to the United States concerning Soviet achievements in avionics and weaponry. Alex was the solution to that problem. Whenever an important new development came up, the two men simply exchanged places. Alex functioned in Major Kotosvk's place while the major was in the States assisting the Americans in duplicating and studying the Soviet equipment. Meanwhile,

Alex was gaining more valuable information, as well as firsthand experience with the Soviet equipment in its native habitat.

The first time they exchanged places, Major Kotosvk was the captain of an Antonov AN-12 transport aircraft that flew into Sofia, Bulgaria. Alex was waiting in the restroom at the airport when Major Kotosvk entered. Even though the two men had never met, they were so thoroughly briefed on each other, they experienced an instant bond. They quickly exchanged clothing and identities. Five minutes later, Alex walked out as Major Grigori Kotosvk. Kotosvk then boarded the civilian airliner for Paris, using Alex's passport. Alex entered the cockpit of the Soviet transport, and seated himself in the Captain's seat. He had never flown that type of aircraft before, though he had spent several hours in a mockup familiarizing himself with the instrument panel. Telling the copilot he didn't feel well, Alex sat back and watched the other two crew members perform the pre-flight and engine start routine.

The copilot, thankful for the opportunity to fly, performed the takeoff as Alex watched. By the time they arrived at Moscow, Alex had observed enough to feel comfortable making the landing. The months of preparation for this mission had been so thorough Alex slipped into his personification of Major Kotosvk quite easily.

The Major was a bachelor with no close friends or family members, so there were no particularly close identity calls. By the second or third day, most of Alex's apprehension was gone. He was to undergo training on a newly introduced model of the MIG-23. Because of his test pilot experience the training was a piece of cake and Alex performed exceptionally well. He wondered how Major Kotosvk would do when he returned in a few weeks and had to fly the MIG himself without having had the benefit of the training. He hoped the major was flexible.

Now, sitting on the flight from Phoenix back to Dallas, Alex couldn't help but wonder why he was thinking of his days in Russia. He had impersonated Major Kotosvk on numerous occasions before the major was killed in an airplane crash. Alex felt a personal loss when it had happened. Living in the man's shoes, Alex came to admire and respect him. He often wondered if the crash would have been prevented had Kotosvk participated in the training Alex had received in his place. Alex was certain the crash was not an accident, but the work of a young, very aggressive KGB captain, Veektor Zhukov.

Zhukov was onto Alex, and came very close to uncovering him. He arranged a hearing in which he intended to expose Alex as an American spy. Among his "evidence" was a film strip of Alex transmitting Soviet secrets to a known American messenger. In the filmed sequence, Zhukov managed to capture Alex in various situations in which brief slips in his mannerisms and appearance strongly indicated he was not Kotosvk, but an imposter.

Fortunately, Alex managed to get his hands on the film strip the night before the hearing. Using his skills in embedding subliminal suggestive messages, the American doctored the film. He doctored it so well, in fact, even Zhukov was subtly duped into believing Alex Davis was not only Grigori Kotosvk, but was a Soviet patriot to the highest degree. Such was the skill Alex had learned in the use of subliminal communication via film, thanks to CAFI's training. Zhukov was fooled at the time, but later he apparently realized he had been tricked. By arranging the killing of Kotosvk, Zhukov apparently convinced himself he was permanently rid of the American spy who had made a fool of him in front of his superiors.

All of that was years behind now. To get CAFI off his mind, Alex turned to Bud Ewing and discussed with him some of the modifications that would need to be made to the Windecker Eagle in order for it to suit their purposes.

4

Two weeks passed. Alex called to check on the Windecker Eagle's progress almost every day. Because he sensed no more intrusion from CAFI, he began to think his suspicions about the agency's attempts to influence him had been his imagination after all.

He had an occasion to check on some business interests in San Antonio and he and Susan flew down in the Cessna 182. They spent Tuesday night in the Alamo City just for the fun of it. In the evening, they walked along the River Walk and listened to a jazz band at a sidewalk cafe. For just a brief moment, Alex thought of going to see J. L. McDaniels while he was in town. Because Susan was with him and because he had perceived no futher interference, he decided against it. Alex was more at ease than he had been in weeks. He and Susan enjoyed the time together away from the children and the hectic pace which was so much a part of their lives in Dallas.

Wednesday morning they slept late. That afternoon they flew back to Dallas. Ken Webb was in Dallas on Thursday and Friday and the three men spent most of the two days in planning sessions with members of their technical staff. Late Friday afternoon, Alex called Phoenix to see if the plane was ready and was told the inspections were estimated to be completed Saturday around noon. He made reservations to fly out on an American Airlines flight early Saturday morning.

The Eagle was ready by mid-afternoon on Saturday. Alex checked the weather for the flight home and found he had clear skies and a good tailwind most of the way. He planned for a fuel stop in El Paso, and expected to arrive home around midnight.

As Alex departed the Sun City Airport in the Windecker Eagle, the first thing he noticed about the airplane was that it was extremely noisy inside the cockpit. The plane would definitely need some soundproofing before it was used for much cross-country travel. As the flight progressed, Alex checked the radios and navigation equipment to determine what was worth keeping. He and Bud had already discussed having the avionics panel completely redone with modern radios. They would need to make some modifications to the instrument panel anyway in order to mount the new disponder.

The Eagle gave Alex a good, solid 160 knot cruise. With the tailwind, he was making a little over 200 knots groundspeed. The cabin was comfortable, with seating for four. This particular airplane had been fitted with a good grade of blue fabric seats that had worn well. The composite airframe was of a material which grew stronger with age. The plane had a good feel to it. In fact, except for the noise, it was very comfortable to fly.

Alex landed at El Paso a little after dark. He went into the airport restaurant and had a hamburger while the aircraft was being refueled. After eating, Alex rechecked the weather. Skies were still clear in the Dallas area. The flight to Dallas took three and a half hours.

Before leaving Dallas, Alex had tried to arrange for a hangar at Addison Airport for the Windecker, but was unsucessful. Upon landing at Addison, Alex taxied the Eagle to the hangar where the Cessna 182 was kept. He pulled the 182 out of the hangar and tied it down on the ramp. Then he parked the Eagle in its place.

Susan was still awake when Alex got home. "How was your flight?" she asked.

"It was a nice flight, Susan. The weather was beautiful and I had a good tailwind." He sat down on the edge of the bed to remove his shoes. "I sure am tired, though. It could be because the plane is noisy. It doesn't have an autopilot, either, so I had to fly the whole way."

"How about a hot bath?" she asked.

"Sounds great."

Alex was sure when his head hit the pillow, he would fall asleep right away, especially after soaking in a hot bath. But it didn't happen. His body was too tired to unwind and his mind was going a hundred miles an hour. He relived the day's events, thinking back over the early morning flight to Phoenix, the pre-flight of the Eagle, and the long flight back to Dallas. In his mind, he planned the airplane's new instrument panel. He mentally removed all of the door panels to put soundproofing behind them. He tried to decide what type of autopilot they should put in the plane. He thought about having the interior reupholstered and then decided it was unnecessary. Then his mind turned to Bud's pet project and he thought about how little involvement he had in it. He decided the project should get some more of his time. Bud had indicated he would need Alex to fly the test missions.

Alex wasn't sure what time he finally drifted off to sleep, but it was mid-morning when he awoke. Susan's side of the bed was empty. Since it was Sunday, he figured Susan and the kids had gone to church and he wondered why they hadn't awakened him to go with them. There was a note on the table by the bed.

> *The kids and I have gone to church. You seemed so tired, I didn't want to wake you.*
>
> *Karen called this morning, and said she needs to see you urgently. She wants you to come over when you can. She arrived home early this morning.*
>
> *Love, Susan*

Alex took a shower, hoping to get some of the stiffness out of his body. He shaved and put on his jogging suit. Karen's car was at his house. He would drive it over and worry about how to get home later.

Alex turned into Karen's driveway and drove around to the back of the house. Getting out of the car, he walked through the patio gate to the double glass doors leading to the kitchen. The housekeeper, Consuelo, met him at the back door. "Miss Karen's asleep upstairs, Mr. Davis. She's pretty tired, but she wanted me to wake her if you came by."

Thank you, Consuelo. What time did she get home?"

"She got to the airport about 7:00 this morning. She was on the plane from London all night."

"Maybe I should just let her sleep."

"No, sir. She made me promise I would get her up when you got here. I think she really wants to talk to you."

"Okay. If that's what she wants."

Consuelo headed upstairs to get Karen while Alex went to the refrigerator to get a couple of Cokes. He figured Karen would want one when she came down. He was rummaging around for something to make some sandwiches out of when Karen appeared, wearing a pair of gray slacks and a sweatshirt. She looked groggy. Consuelo was right behind her and when she saw Alex in front of the refrigerator, she pushed herself past Karen and started scolding him. "Now, Mr. Davis, you visit with Dr. Webster. I'll get you all something to eat." Alex smiled and stepped out of the way, sufficiently chastised for making himself at home in Consuelo's kitchen.

"I'm so glad you're here, Alex," Karen said. "What time is it?" She looked around the kitchen for a clock, as if she were in an unfamiliar place. She had been gone for a while, and her body was on a different schedule.

"I think it's around noon. You look really tired."

"I am, but I want you to see something."

She beckoned him to follow her as she walked through the dining area into the library. There she located her purse in a chair, rummaged around in it, and came up with an envelope. She handed it to Alex.

"What's this?" he asked.

"It's a letter that was given to me while I was in Moscow. It's written in Russian. I think it's important."

Alex pulled the contents out of the envelope. The library was dark, so he walked over to a window and opened the blinds. He was holding a handwritten letter three pages long. The handwriting was bold and in some places, difficult to read.

Alex sank into a chair. Karen was right. The letter was written in Russian, and though Alex's command of the language was very good, the message in the letter was not clear to him. He read it over twice and decided it was either highly technical in an area unfamiliar to him, or it was encrypted, or both.

He looked up at Karen, who was eagerly awaiting his explanation. "I don't understand this, Karen. It appears to be pretty technical."

"Would writing it out help?"

"Maybe. It's possible if I translate it, some of it will make sense to you."

Karen opened a desk drawer and pulled out a pen and some paper. Alex shook his head as she offered them to him. "I'd rather use the computer." He sat down at her desk and turned on her PC. When it came up, he clicked on the word processor icon and started typing. Karen stood over his shoulder for a minute or two, but thinking she might be bothering him, moved to her recliner to wait. Alex typed quickly as he translated some parts of the text. Other parts were more difficult and he labored over them.

Karen waited patiently for a few minutes, but seeing Alex would probably be awhile, she slipped out to the kitchen to get the drinks and sandwiches Consuelo had fixed for them. Alex was so absorbed he didn't even notice Karen leave. When she came back into the library with the food, Alex was still concentrating on the letter. Finally, he looked up at her and shrugged his shoulders as he sent the document to the printer.

"I hope you understand this," he said, handing her the pages as they came off the printer, "because I sure don't."

Karen took the printed sheets of paper from Alex and sat back in her recliner. "Help yourself." She motioned toward the food she had set down on the corner of the desk. Alex picked up a sandwich and began to munch as Karen read.

She read the document carefully, reading some sections two or three times.

"Alex, this is fascinating," she said, finally. "If this is what it appears to be, it may well be the medical breakthrough we have been looking for, for a long time!"

"What do you mean?"

"I mean this looks like a successful and relatively inexpensive cure for cancer."

"But why give it to you on three scribbled sheets of paper? Why not publish it to the world?"

She sounded impatient. "Oh, Alex, don't you see? This isn't it; it's not the cure itself. This is just enough information to let me know the man who gave it to me, Dr. Orgutsov, really has the cure and he wants to make it available to us."

"Okay, so why not give you the real thing?"

"You know his government would never go for that. They would find some way to exploit it, or make everyone pay dearly for the cure."

"What makes you think that, Karen? Surely the medical profession and its concern for humanity is beyond the new Kremlin's political games."

"I'm afraid not, Alex. You should have seen how they treated those of us from outside the country. It was obvious they wanted to get any information from us they could while giving us nothing in return. Their physicians were so closely guarded it was a minor miracle Dr. Orgutsov was able to get this information to me."

"How did he do it?"

"He didn't give it to me himself. In fact, I'm not real sure how he managed it. There was a set of handouts that apparently had the Party's approval. They were stacked in a chair for us to pick up. When I walked over to get mine, the official guarding the stack stopped me and handed me one he was holding instead. I didn't discover the letter inside it until later."

"So there might have been others who got the same letter?"

"I don't think so. I watched most of them flip through the handouts during the session. I'm relatively certain mine was the only one that had something in it. That official must have had something to do with it. I surmised it had come from Dr. Orgutsov because I saw him watching me until he was sure I had seen the letter. Then he nodded at me as if to say, 'It's in your hands now'."

"Then it seems you were chosen, Karen. There was some reason Doctor what's-his-name singled you out to know about his discovery."

"Dr. Orgutsov, Alex. He is probably one of the most known and respected physicians in all of Russia. I don't imagine he has ever even heard of me. I had very little contact with him at the conference. How could he possibly have chosen me?"

"Because he knew you would do something with it. What is it anyway? What do all of these formulas mean? And this last part here looks like some kind of itinerary. Those are cities. I'm familiar with most of them. And those are dates and times beside the cities."

Alex was looking at the original set of papers while he talked. Karen was still holding the translated version in her hands. As far as he was concerned, most of the document was filled with technical stuff which meant nothing to him. He wondered if Karen really understood what she was seeing, and if so, he marveled at her education. Alex had a pretty good engineering background from his test pilot days, but this wasn't like anything he had ever seen.

Karen sat at her desk and pulled out some reference books. She thumbed through some pages, read a little, and referred to the translated document from time to time. She busied herself there for several minutes without looking up. Alex ate his sandwich and watched Karen work. Whatever it was she was on to was certainly capturing her attention. She hardly touched her food. Finally, Karen stood up, walked over to Alex and sat on the arm of his chair. "Alex, Dr. Orgutsov has been working with lasers and a chemical very similar to the InterLeukin that has been making headlines here. According to what these documents show, he has had nearly a one hundred percent success rate in treating cancer in all stages of growth and in all parts of the body."

"What do you mean a hundred percent?"

"Just that, Alex. His cure works and he has proven it over and over."

"Yeah, so he says, but can you trust him?"

"Alex, that's why he wants us to know about it. Yes, I trust him. I can tell enough from what he has given me here that he knows what he is doing. And he's talking about a cure without side effects. No nausea, no loss of hair, no impairment of the digestive process. This is wonderful!"

"Okay, so you take the information he has given you and you start curing cancer patients and you're the hero. He just handed wealth and fame into your lap."

"It's not that simple," she said a little impatiently. "He didn't give me the cure. There's no way he could do that without being here. The chemical has to be manufactured using the body's own immune cells as a base. I don't know the technique, and it's too complex to communicate on three pieces of paper. Then there are the lasers. The exact frequency composition and the temperature of the laser beam are critical and they vary according to the size and nature of the tumors being treated." Karen was looking at Alex as if she wanted something from him, as if she wanted him to say something, to do something.

Alex caught the tone. "Then what's the point in what he gave you?"

"The point is, Al, he wants us to get him out."

"Out of Russia?"

"Yes."

"What do you mean, 'us'? What have we got to do with it?"

"It's obvious Dr. Orgutsov doesn't trust the cure to his own government. I don't know whether they know about it or not, but you can bet he hasn't released his entire secret to them. The Soviets wouldn't share that cure with anyone. They would find some way to blackmail everyone with it. But if we have the cure, we'll make it available to the entire world. I believe Orgutsov wants to bring his cure to the United States so it can be available to anyone who needs it."

"You got all of that from those three pieces of paper?" Alex was skeptical.

"Not entirely. I got some of it from the paper. I also got some of it from being around the doctor in his own country. Some of it is just a feeling I have, but what cinches it is the itinerary."

"Yeah, I wondered about that, too, Karen. It seems out of place ... unless he expects you to do something with it."

"Exactly. But what, I don't know."

"Me neither, but I know one thing. You'd better get some sleep. Especially if you are going back to work tomorrow. I'd hate to have a doctor with severe jet lag cutting on me."

"You're right, Alex. Call me tomorrow if you get a chance. I need to think about this for a while."

Karen hugged Alex and kissed him on the cheek as he stood to leave. He needed to get away for a while, to think this thing through himself. Getting a prominent Soviet physician out of the new Soviet Union would be no easy task, especially if the current power regime didn't want him to go. You can bet if they had even the remotest idea of what he was involved in, they wouldn't let him out of the country. If Karen's reasoning was correct, Alex needed to figure out who they should go to with this information.

Karen headed upstairs to go back to bed. Alex remembered he had driven over in her car, so he used the phone in the kitchen to call Susan. She had just gotten home from church and said she would come pick him up. While he was waiting for Susan, Alex looked around Karen's library for an atlas. Finding one, he sat down in the recliner and turned the pages, looking for a map of the Soviet Union. Karen's atlas was outdated, but the country names and borders in the new Soviet Union closely matched those of the original USSR, the one before the democratic reforms of the early part of the decade.

The Soviet Union was broken down into three different maps. The first map was of the Baltic and Moscow regions. Alex was not interested in that part of the country. Turning to the next page, he found a map of Western and Central Soviet Union. Comparing Dr. Orgutsov's itinerary to the map, he began to trace the doctor's planned route. The itinerary included cities such as Sverdlovsk, Petropaviovsk, Omsk, Novosibirsk, Krasnojarsk, Irkutsk, Cita and Jakutsk. The last three cities were found on the third page, which was a map of the Eastern part of the Soviet Union. Most of the cities listed were familiar to Alex from his time spent as a pilot in the Soviet Air Force. The route seemed to follow the Trans-Siberian railroad. The dates indicated by each city were appropriate for travel by train. From what Alex could gather, the doctor was making visits to each of these cities, probably on some kind of government-sponsored tour.

The trip would cover several weeks. Russia is a big country and their trains aren't super trains like the ones in Japan or Europe.

Alex looked up and saw Susan through the patio window. He went to the kitchen door to meet her. "Where's Karen?" Susan asked as Alex opened the door for her.

"She's upstairs asleep. Where are Paul and Mary?"

"They're in the car. They wanted to see what Karen brought them, but I thought she might be tired, so I wouldn't let them come in."

"We'll have her over to dinner one night this week," Alex said. "She can tell them all about her trip then."

"They'll love that. They want to know if we can go out to eat, then drive out to the airport and fly in the new plane?"

"Sure," Alex said, "that sounds like fun."

They started toward the car. "You've got to tell me what it was Karen had to see you about so urgently," Susan said.

5

Alex had a hard time keeping his own mind off the letter. That CAFI was behind the letter, or at least knew about it, Alex was almost certain. Was Karen involved because of McDaniels' relationship with her? Were they dragging her into whatever it was they wanted him to do?

Alex had operated independently when he was with the intelligence agency. The risks were too great to be involving others. He had kept Susan out of danger by bowing out of CAFI soon after their marriage. As far as Karen's knowledge of what he had done, she had only known he was involved in undercover work, but no details. She never had any firsthand knowledge of his missions. The web entangling him against his wishes was tightening and now it was including Karen. Alex was more determined than ever to guard against them, but felt helpless.

No matter how he looked at it or what he believed, the Russian doctor, his discovery and his itinerary was intriguing. Alex didn't know how to judge the importance of the doctor's discovery, but Karen did, and Alex trusted Karen's judgment in matters of medicine. He wanted her to decide the contents of the letter were insignificant, but doubted that would be the case. If it really was what it appeared to be, and if Karen was correct in her assessment about the Soviets exploiting the discovery, then extracting the Russian doctor from his country was the right thing to do—providing the doctor really wanted to leave, that is.

Karen believed that was what he was trying to tell her in the letter, but how could she be so sure? The only way Alex would know would be to talk to the doctor directly. But, if he could get close enough to talk to him, he had better be ready to get him out of the country. Alex was thinking all of this through while driving his family to the airport. He suddenly realized Susan had been talking to him.

"I'm sorry, Susan, I was thinking. What were you saying?"

"You weren't listening," she said with a bit of exasperation. "You're in your own world somewhere. You act as if you're not even here with us. I was asking you where we were going to eat."

"Oh. I'd forgotten about eating. Consuelo fixed me a sandwiche when I was at Karen's."

"Well, we didn't eat and we're starving."

"Okay. How about Wendy's? There's one right up here on Beltline Road."

"That's fine." Susan tried not to be irritated, but it came out in her voice.

Susan resented Alex's detachment. Sometimes it seemed he just tuned them out. Lately it was happening frequently. He didn't seem to notice when Paul and Mary were getting into it with each other. She wished he would take more notice of what the kids were doing and help her with them. She had to be with them all the time and it was obvious they needed more discipline than they were getting.

Normally, Alex was a good husband and father and Susan didn't have much to complain about. She was angry with herself when she did get down on him, but sometimes she just needed some relief. She could feel a barrier coming between them today and she was determined not to let it happen. It was in her hands right now. She could nag at him for all of the little things bothering her, or she could move in close to him—emotionally as well as physically—and tear down the wall before it could be built. She reached for Alex's hand and squeezed it. He couldn't retreat in defense if she wasn't on the attack.

Alex found Susan's gesture a welcome relief. He already felt guilty about having his mind elsewhere. If he could change the way he was, he would gladly do it. He decided to force the whole matter of the letter out of his mind and give himself to his family for the rest of the day.

He hoped Susan would forget to follow up on what it was that Karen had needed to see him about so urgently.

Wendy's was just ahead and Alex turned in. After the family had ordered, they sat at a table near the window and Alex concentrated on being there for his family—mentally, as well as physically. Susan recognized his effort to put everything but his family out of his mind, so she didn't ask about his visit to Karen's.

After lunch, they pulled the Windecker Eagle out of the hangar and went for a ride. It was a beautiful afternoon. They flew up to Lake Texoma and back. Alex still didn't like the noise of the plane, but he knew what needed to be done to fix that. They got back before dark and Alex took Paul to play racquetball. Paul was eight and just learning to play, but he really enjoyed the time spent with his dad. They played for about an hour, swam for a few minutes in the pool at the health club, then went home. Susan fixed bacon and eggs for supper.

The sun went down and with it, Alex's resolve to not be involved. The phone rang and he expected it to be Karen. When it wasn't he was disappointed.

Sleep didn't come easy that night. Alex's mind was full of plans he felt he shouldn't be making. If getting Dr. Orgutsov out of Russia was something that really needed to be done, then Alex knew he was the man to do it. He knew it, yet he didn't want to admit it. Nevertheless, he found himself mentally formulating plans that would be necessary should such a mission become a reality. He finally drifted off to sleep sometime in the wee hours of the morning.

Monday was an extremely busy day. So busy, in fact, Alex had practically no time to think about the events of the day before. A major contract, this one with a non-government customer, was in jeopardy. The contract was crucial if the business was ever going to gain the long-term stability it needed. Alex, Bud and Ken recognized the need to place more of their business in the private sector since the government budgeting process was undergoing such scrutiny. The majority of their government contracts in recent years had been of the speculative, high-tech variety.

The businessmen knew their products were good and were priced fairly. However, convincing congressional committees of that was not always easy. They had turned to major aircraft and electronics manufacturers as a market for some of their newest products.

Today, Ken had been calling from Memphis with new information every fifteen minutes. Alex and Bud had to act on the information and stay in touch with the top managers within the organization. The working relationship was not in jeopardy, rather a major misunderstanding had arisen in the expected capabilities of the product. Compromise was the only answer, yet neither side had much room to compromise. Late in the afternoon, Bud asked Alex to fly with him to St. Louis for a face-to-face meeting. Ken would meet them there.

Alex called Susan to tell her he was leaving town. Then he called Karen's office. She was with a patient and couldn't come to the phone. The receptionist promised to get a message to her as soon as possible. Alex had to leave before Karen returned his call. He told his secretary to tell her where he would be staying in St. Louis, even though he knew they would be in meetings until well into the night.

They rushed to the airport and Alex was somewhat relieved when he and Bud were unable to get adjacent seats. He needed at least an hour or two of sleep before heading into a late night negotiating session. He fell asleep and dreamed of flights over the ocean and over mountain ranges. In his dreams, he didn't have a map. The land below him, as he flew along in his dream world, was familiar. When he awoke, he realized he had been flying over the Soviet Union and it wasn't a MIG, or a Hound or any of the other Soviet aircraft he had been flying. It was the Windecker Eagle.

The business meeting lasted until well after midnight. Before going up to his room, Alex checked for messages at the hotel desk. There had been no call from Karen. Perhaps she had decided the letter wasn't so important after all. That night he slept well and woke up the next morning refreshed. He had breakfast with Bud and Ken. Most of the issues concerning the contract had been settled the night before. Ken was going to stay on and work out the details. Alex and Bud headed back to Dallas on a morning flight. They were at DFW Airport before lunch and went to the office ready to work. Bud went to the engineering lab to check on his projects; Alex went to his office to catch up on paperwork. There were no calls from Karen. Alex called Susan and told her he was back in town and would be home for dinner. Susan informed him Karen was coming to dinner.

As Alex hung up the telephone receiver, the doubts began again. Karen was coming to dinner. Ordinarily that would have been a treat. She would tell them about her trip. A born storyteller, Karen was always interesting to be around and the kids loved her. But the fact she had been communicating with Susan during the past two days and not with Alex made him wonder what she might have told Susan about the letter. Or would she say something about it tonight?

Karen would know Alex did not want Susan to know about the letter. She knew how important it was for Alex to protect Susan from the knowledge of CAFI. But just the fact she would be there and they couldn't talk about it would be a problem.

Alex began to pace the office. CAFI was getting to him. It was this Russian doctor business. They were behind it all, they had been preparing Alex, they had used Karen as a messenger and now they were making it impossible for him to get it off his mind. The Windecker Eagle was probably part of the plan. He had fallen into that one so easily. Alex had wanted the Eagle like a kid wants the latest toy he sees advertised on television. Now he was thinking of ways the Eagle could be used to get the Russian doctor to the United States. But that was a ridiculous idea—fly a civilian single engine plane into the Soviet Union, pick up an important Soviet citizen and fly back out of the country with him. Right! Come on, Alex, you're dreaming.

Alex went to Bud's office to see if he had come back from the shop. He found him seated at his desk looking at some technical drawings. "Bud," Alex said. "I've been thinking about the Eagle. I would like to fly it over to Fort Worth to the radio shop this afternoon and get them started on installing the new avionics."

"Fine, Alex. Just make sure they leave a three-inch high, standard-width slot for the prototype of the disponder. I'll need a DB-25 connector with 24 volts supplied to it and an additional transponder antenna mounted just behind the regular one on the airplane's belly."

"So, you decided you're going to stick with the disponder name?" Alex asked.

"Yeah; why not? It displaces, scrambles and multiplies the transponder signals. We'll think of another name for it before we put it into production if we need to. It will probably wind up with some secret code name from the military anyway."

"Bud, I started looking at the engineering specs after our conversation the other day. I've got some questions, but I've got too much going on right now to get into it."

"No problem, Alex. The concept is really quite simple and you'll understand it once I explain it to you. Let's hope our Russian buddies don't get wind of it though. If they knew how it worked, they could unscramble the signals in a jiffy and it would be just like a regular transponder to them. They could zero right in on whatever plane was using it. See you later."

Alex got one of the company employees to drive him to the airport then head for Meacham Field in Fort Worth to pick him up. It would take him about an hour for the driver to get there. Alex would make it in about ten minutes. If Karen was coming to dinner, they probably would not eat until 7:00 o'clock or later, so he would have plenty of time to make sure the radio shop foreman understood what they wanted in the Eagle.

Alex planned to have a standard King Silver Crown radio package installed, plus a Stormscope for helping to detect thunderstorms and turbulence, and a Loran for navigation. He still had not decided on an autopilot. He doubted if one had ever been certified for the Windecker and if not, the certification process would take some time. That would have to come later.

It was after six when Alex got home. He went to take a shower and change clothes before Karen arrived. Susan was busy in the kitchen. Paul and Mary were watching television. The letter had been on Alex's mind the entire afternoon. In the shower, he made up his mind. If the Russian doctor was real, he would get him out—he alone. He knew he had to make up his mind before it was made up for him. Tonight he had to find out from Karen if it was real or not. One way or another, the decision was made. If it was real, he would go. If this was what CAFI wanted, he would take away from them the satisfaction of coercing him into going. Tonight it would be his decision and they would have nothing to do with it. Or would they? His resolve seemed to go down the drain with the last of the shower water. Had it been his decision or not? As he was dressing, he heard the kids run to the door. Karen had arrived. *Some spy,* he thought. *Can't even make a decisive decision.*

Karen kept Susan and the kids entertained throughout the meal and into the evening with stories about her trip. Never once was the letter mentioned. When it was time for her to go, Alex walked her to the car. "Karen," he asked, "what about the doctor? Is he real?"

"He's real, Alex."

"Are you sure he wants out?"

"No question about it."

"Then I'll get him."

"Of course you will, and I'm going with you."

"No you aren't. It's out of the question."

"There's no question about it. Alex, you don't even know Dr. Orgutsov and he doesn't know you. I have to go with you. I'm the contact point."

Karen was talking about an undercover, highly dangerous trip into the Soviet Union as if it were a trip to the beach. She obviously had no comprehension of what such a mission would entail. She had some crazy idea about a spy-novel type of adventure that was nothing like real life. There was no way he would let her be involved. Then again, there was no one he trusted more. If he needed to count on someone for help, Karen could be counted on. But she meant too much to Alex for him to let her life be endangered. Alex put his hands on Karen's shoulders and looked her straight in the eyes. "Absolutely not."

Karen just smiled back at him, opened her car door and got in. "Good night, Alex. Let's get together tomorrow night and start working on a plan." She started the Mercedes and backed out of the driveway, leaving Alex staring after her.

Back in his study, Alex settled into the comfort of his recliner. Susan came in and asked if she could get anything for him. "No thanks, hon," he said. "I just want to sit here for a while." She left to make sure the kids were in bed. Alex shifted fully into the planning mode. He was a natural at planning a mission like this and his experience with CAFI had sharpened his natural talents. Even though it had been years, he found he still had the knack. He knew what needed to be done; he only had to work out the details. But he was bothered by the fact that the best plan he could come up with, the only one he was relatively certain would work, involved Karen. He kept trying to find an alternate plan, but couldn't settle on but one plan he believed would work.

He made a mental list of the things he would need to do to prepare for the mission. The doctor's travel itinerary began in less than a month. That didn't leave much time. Part of the preparation had begun already— having new avionics installed in the Eagle. He would have to go to New Orleans, preferably sometime this week. He wondered if he could still get into the center there. It was possible the contacts had changed. Perhaps he should check with J. L. McDaniels to see what changes had taken place. Alex hated to give McDaniels the satisfaction of knowing he was going to take the mission, yet he could at least rest in the fact he had decided on his own. He had not been coerced through any of CAFI's tricks. Well, he didn't think he had.

Alex picked up his phone and once again dialed the contact number—the one he had remembered from years earlier. He followed the procedure exactly as he remembered it from frequent use when he was an active agent. Everything happened as it should until he entered his four-digit code. Once again, he got the same results. Instead of a voice on the other end of the line, he got a dial tone. He quickly redialed the number, and got the same results again. So, Alex thought, I guess McDaniels has changed his contact procedure. Maybe the center in New Orleans was no longer there, either. But it didn't belong to CAFI. It was a joint use center of all the intelligence agencies. Agents were identified at the center by voice print and fingerprints. Surely things would be the same at the center.

Alex turned off the light in his den and went upstairs to bed. Susan was already there. He reached for her under the covers and she snuggled close. The faint smell of perfume answered the question on his mind.

Wednesday morning Alex busied himself in the office. He dictated several letters, went through his mail and placed a call to Andy Young. Andy ran a small aircraft maintenance shop at Addison Airport and did all the maintenance on Alex's Cessna. "Andy, this is Alex Davis. What do you know about a Windecker Eagle?"

"Just what I've read, Mr. Davis. I don't know that I've ever seen one."

"DEW, Inc. just bought one and I need you to do some modifications to it for me. Do you think you could do some research on it?"

"Yes, sir. What do you want done?"

"I need long-range fuel tanks in it, as much fuel as possible, even if it includes ferry tanks. It also needs soundproofing in the cabin walls, and I'd like to get it modified to use autogas. It has a Continental 285 engine in it."

"I doubt any Supplemental Type Certificate exists for that airplane, Mr. Davis. We'll have to go through the certification process to make it legal."

"That's all right, Andy. We'll just fly it in the experimental category while we're waiting on certification. I'll worry about that part if you'll take care of the mechanics of it."

"Where is the airplane? I'll need to look at it."

"It's in Fort Worth at the radio shop. I'll have it back at Addison by Monday."

"Okay. Meanwhile, I'll do some reading to see what I can find out."

"Thanks, Andy."

"Don't mention it."

The next call Alex made was to his travel agency. He made reservations on a Delta flight to New Orleans late that afternoon with a return flight the next afternoon. Then he called Susan and told her he was going to New Orleans for the night.

"New Orleans?" Susan said. "You haven't been there in a while. I didn't know DEW, Inc. had any customers around New Orleans."

"We don't," Alex replied.

"Then why are you going?" she asked. It had started already. Alex didn't want to lie to Susan, but he couldn't tell her the truth, either. He could only hope she wouldn't ask too many questions. He would have to ask her to trust him and he wouldn't be able to tell her why. These next few weeks might put a strain on their marriage. He would have a number of unexplained absences. He just hoped it would all be over before Susan began to get too uncomfortable with him not being able to include her in what he was doing.

"Susan, it's just something I've got to tend to. I'll be home tomorrow afternoon."

"Bye. I love you, Alex." She hung up. Her voice was cold, even though the words were warm. Alex slowly put down the receiver. Hurting Susan was something he didn't like to do. He started to call her back, but what could he say that wouldn't raise more questions?

Later that afternoon, Alex rented a car at Moissant Airport in New Orleans and drove to the Holiday Inn in Metairie. He went to a seafood restaurant for dinner, then went back to his room and watched TV. He wondered what Karen was doing. He remembered she had wanted to get together that night and plan their mission. He started to call her to tell her he was out of town, but didn't want to let her know what he was doing. It went against his grain to stand her up, but they had not made a definite commitment. Karen would call the house and Susan would tell her Alex had left town.

The next morning after breakfast, Alex drove to the French Quarter. He turned up Rampart Street, three blocks east of Canal Street, and entered the parking lot of the Dauphine-Orleans Hotel. Parking the car, he crossed the street and walked towards the Wax Museum. At the corner of Conti and Dauphine Streets, he entered a courtyard. After climbing the stairs to a balcony overlooking the courtyard, he stopped at the second door—a solid wooden door with no markings. He tried the knob and the door opened. On the far side of the room stood a counter, much like a bar. Behind the counter hung a curtain. No one was in sight. Alex walked over and placed his hands on the countertop. It looked like wood, but was made of a synthetic material. Alex spoke his name. "Alex Davis." From behind the curtain a door opened and an oriental man appeared. "Hello, Phuoc," Alex said.

"Hello, Alex. It has been awhile."

"I didn't know if this place would still be here. I certainly didn't expect to see you still around," Alex said.

"Some things never change," Phuoc responded. If you hadn't still been in the computer for a voice and fingerprint ID, then I wouldn't be here—just this empty room."

"Well, I'm here and you're here, and I've got a list."

"Figured you did. This is not the kind of place where you just drop in for a visit. Come on in and give me your list."

Alex followed Phuoc through the door behind the curtain. As soon as they entered the adjoining room, the door closed behind them. Phuoc handed Alex a clipboard with a yellow legal pad attached to it. The shopping lists agents brought in here were seldom written down. Phuoc preferred to work from a written list. Many times he could fill the order on the spot. Sometimes it took him a day or so. Whenever he finished, the list would be given back to the requesting agent who would destroy it.

There were never any accounting records kept here as far as Alex could tell. He wondered who funded the place and how the various intelligence agencies got charged for their goods. The place was literally a spy shop. It specialized in disguises, forged identity papers, passports and visas, as well as a number of James Bond-type gadgets. Alex had found the shop very useful during his days with CAFI. He was slightly amused to find himself there again, but he didn't feel at all uncomfortable. He jotted down a number of items on the pad and handed it back to the oriental.

Phuoc looked at the list. "Routine stuff," he said. "What age will the Russian woman be?"

"Forty," Alex replied.

Phuoc handed him a stack of photographs. "Pick one," he said. Alex studied the photographs, then handed back his choice. "I'll have this stuff ready in a few minutes, Alex. You want a cup of coffee while you wait?"

"No," Alex replied, "but I'll take a Coke if you have one."

"In the fridge." Phuoc motioned toward a refrigerator that stood against the south wall of the room. Alex walked over and, opening the door, found a Coke on the bottom shelf. He stood looking out the window overlooking Dauphine Street. The traffic below was slow because of the time of day. There were a few people walking up and down the street looking into the shop windows. Probably out-of-towners, Alex thought.

Forty-five minutes later, Phuoc handed Alex a briefcase with a combination lock. Alex thanked the man and turned toward the door. He walked out onto the balcony and down the stairs to the street. Instead of going back the way he had come, he walked around the block to Burgandy Street. He entered the side entrance of the hotel and used a pay phone in the hall to call home. There was no answer. He called Karen's office. The receptionist said Karen was at the hospital. Alex called his office and talked to Bud Ewing. "Where are you, Alex? Andy Young has been trying to call you, Karen Webster has called twice, and Ken needs you in Memphis. He thought he had the St. Louis deal closed up but they raised some questions only you can answer."

"Okay, I'll call Ken. I'm in New Orleans. I had to make a quick trip down here on personal business. If Ken needs me there, I can fly to Memphis from here."

"Good. Give him a call. What do I tell Andy or Karen if they call again?"

"Tell them I'll be back tonight or in the morning. There's nothing they need that can't wait that long."

"Right. See you tomorrow," Bud replied.

Alex called Ken and learned he was needed in Memphis. There was a Delta ticket counter in the hotel lobby, so Alex walked over and had his ticket changed. There was a flight to Memphis right after lunch he could easily make. He drove back to the airport, turned in his car and went to the departure

83

gate for his flight. He had about an hour to wait, so he bought a paperback. He tried to read, but kept thinking about the task that was before him. Some of the items on the shopping list he had given Phuoc assumed Karen would be going with him. He did not intend to let Karen be involved, but if it turned out to be the only option that would work, he would be prepared. His lack of resolve disturbed him. Karen could generally talk him into just about anything. He just didn't want it to happen this time.

The crisis in Memphis was minor. Alex had to explain some technical aspects of the product to the customer's engineers and the deal was in the bag again. Somebody had given them some partial information and they had filled in the gaps with some of their own suppositions–suppositions that were incorrect.

Alex arrived back in Dallas a little after 11:00 p.m. He called Susan from the airport to let her know he was in town and would be home in a few minutes. Her voice sounded fine over the phone. She seemed anxious to see him. At home his reception was as if nothing had been wrong between them.

Friday morning, Alex went to his office early, closed the door and opened the briefcase. Alex's birthday was February 28. The combination to the briefcase would have been set by Phuoc as 12-30–two less than the month, two more than the day of his birth. That was something else that hadn't changed over the years. When the case was open, Alex quickly checked its contents: tickets on the Trans-Siberian Railroad, three sets of identity papers, Russian currency and various other items—mostly small, effective items of disguise. There was also an updated list of Soviet military installations, along with their current status and the names of the top ranking officials at each base. After examining the contents, Alex closed the briefcase and put it in the credenza behind his desk. He opened the card file on his desk to find Andy Young's number. Before he could dial the number, the phone rang. It was his direct line. Startled, Alex answered it.

"Alex, it's Karen."

"Good morning, Karen, what are you up to?"

"I'm up to cornering you for lunch, that's what."

"My restaurant, or yours?"

"I'll come there. See you about twelve?"

"That'll be fine."

"Bye, Alex."

"Good-bye, Karen."

Alex hung up the phone and sat back in his chair, an uneasy feeling in his stomach. That was short and sweet—unlike Karen. He was being compelled toward a series of events he didn't want to happen, yet he knew they must. Going into Russia in a civilian airplane to extract a well-known Soviet citizen and bring him to the United States was bad enough. What made it worse was the only plan he could conceive of which had any chance of being successful involved Karen. That was what had Alex so uptight. He didn't fear for his own life. Even though it had been a long time, he had confidence in his ability to pull something off behind the resurrected Iron Curtain. But involving Karen in the mission and insuring her safety was a totally different story. Nevermind she was self-sufficient, and whatever Karen set her mind to, she could, and would, do. He felt a responsibility toward her. For as long as he could remember, Karen had never depended on anyone else for anything. It was probably another one of the reasons she had never married. Maybe she had never met a man strong enough or smart enough for her.

Karen had already determined in her own mind she would be vital to the mission if it was to happen. She seemed to believe it *must* happen. Her life was already dedicated to the healing of mankind. If this was what it appeared to be, she would feel it worth the risk.

Now that Alex had made the decision to undertake the mission, he was somewhat relieved. If CAFI was contacting him through a series of subliminal messages, it could have been them who convinced him to take the challenge. If he made the decision based on Karen's input, that left him in control. The actual planning of the mission would be Alex's. The execution would be Alex's.

What if his motivation was to prove to himself he could still do it? If that was the case, it wasn't worth risking Karen's life or his. He had to decide how he was going to deal with Karen *before* he met her for lunch.

First, he had to call Andy. He dialed Andy Young's number and waited while the phone rang seven or eight times. Andy was most likely on the shop floor working on an airplane. Finally he answered.

"Andy Young Aircraft Repair, Andy speaking."

"Andy, this is Alex Davis."

"Mr. Davis. I have a couple of questions for you."

"Shoot."

"The Windecker, it has a Continental 285 engine."

"That's right."

"That's a fuel-injected engine, Mr. Davis. That engine hasn't been STC'd for autogas."

"Are you sure, Andy? I thought they had even certified a Bonanza for autogas."

"It's not official yet."

"Well find out what you can, and put the same kit on the Eagle they use on a Bonanza. It won't matter if it's certified or not. We'll fly it in the restricted category and get our own STC."

"Okay. About the fuel. How much weight do you need to carry in the cabin with full fuel?"

Alex thought a minute, mentally totaling the weights of his prospective passengers. He allowed 180 pounds for the doctor. He knew Karen weighed about 130, and he weighed almost 200. "Six hundred pounds, Andy."

"That don't allow you much for fuel, Mr. Davis. 'Course that airplane is strong. They tell me that composite material just gets stronger and stronger as it ages. I figure we could probably give you a total of 200 gallons. That would give you about 13 hours in the air, or something like a 2000-mile range."

"Do it, Andy. I'll bring you the airplane Monday."

"Oh, it's already here. Mr. Ewing pick it up yesterday afternoon while you were gone and brought it to me. Evidently, the guys at the radio shop got through with it early."

"They did, huh? Well, okay. I may need to make some more modifications. I'll see you sometime this afternoon."

"Okay, Mr. Davis."

Alex hung up the phone, angry for no reason. He resented that Bud had taken it upon himself to move the Eagle from the radio shop before Alex personally had a chance to check the avionics installation. He took a deep breath to calm himself, and headed down the hall to Ewing's office. When he arrived, he found Bud on the telephone. Ewing motioned for Alex to come in and sit down. Instead, Alex went next door to the restroom. He realized he was getting emotional and that wouldn't help. He stopped at the sink, wet his face and dried it with a paper towel. Catching his image in the mirror, he combed his hair and tucked in his shirttail. Some adventurer, he thought. Alex, you're nothing but a middle-aged, overweight businessman. You'd better forget this spy business. That stuff is long behind you.

Bud was just starting to come out into the hall to look for Alex as he stepped into his office. Bud greeted him cordially. "Morning, Alex. How's everything going?"

"I don't know yet, Bud. Tell me about the Eagle."

"The radio shop called and said they had done everything you wanted them to do. Andy called here a time or two looking for you. He said you had given him a project to work on and he was anxious to get started. I went and got it and took it to him. What is it about that airplane, Alex? You and Andy are both acting like kids in a candy store."

"It's nothing, Bud. It's just the design of that plane is so unique. It really was way ahead of its time. It sure is a shame production on it was so limited."

"Yeah, I guess so. Anyway, I looked at the panel and it has everything we need plus a place to mount the disponder. They did a good job. One thing we forgot, however, is a UHF radio. We'll need that to communicate with the military when we start testing."

"You're right, Bud. I'll talk to one of my buddies over at Collins radio and see what I can do."

"Great," Bud responded.

Alex didn't go back to his office. Instead, he went downstairs and into the computer room. He picked up a printout and then sat at the operator's desk there. No one would bother him and he could think things through before Karen arrived.

Two hours later, Alex was still sitting at the desk when he looked up through the glass wall to see Karen walking toward him. He was no more ready to see her now than he had been when he sat down, but he got up to meet her at the door. "So where do you want to eat?" he asked.

"I'm not really hungry, Alex. It doesn't matter."

"Me neither. Let's just go for a drive or sit in here."

"Staying here is fine. We've got to talk. We're running out of time."

They went back into the computer room. Alex pulled another chair up to the desk and they both sat down. "Alex," Karen began, "I can get back into the country again on a tourist visa. I can take the train and meet up with Dr. Orgutsov somewhere on his itinerary. You've got to figure out where to meet us and how to get us out of the country undetected."

"Whoa, slow down there. We've discussed this before. You don't have any idea the kind of risk you would be taking. If the Soviets discover what you are up to and capture you in their country trying to help one of their citizens defect, they'll put you in prison. The risk is too great, Karen."

"It's worth it, Alex. I've been playing around in the lab with some of Dr. Orgutsov's formulas. I'm convinced he has a cancer cure that works. I also know I can't duplicate it here without him. If there is anything worth taking a risk for, this is it. And you know you can't do it alone. It will be hard enough for me to find him, and I *know* him. You wouldn't stand a chance trying to find him by yourself."

"I was afraid you'd see it that way. That's the same conclusion I had come to, too."

"Of course, Alex. You're definitely no dummy. Now let's get down to business."

They spent the next hour going over the plans Alex had formulated in his mind. He was amazed at how many points in his plan Karen had already figured out for herself. Either they thought alike, or his plan was so simple anyone could have come up with it. He hoped it was the former. Alex knew Karen's presence in the Soviet Union again after such a short period of time would arouse the KGB's curiosity. Yet, if Dr. Orgutsov was not under any suspicion, perhaps they would not associate her with him in any way. But, if they suspected he wanted to defect, then they would be watching him closely and might watch Karen as well. That was a contingency Alex would have to allow for in his plan. They both knew what had to be done. Karen left and Alex tried to get his mind back on work—not an easy task.

During the drive home that evening, Alex mulled over the plans he and Karen had discussed earlier in the day. Her part in the plan was relatively safe if he could pull his part off without a hitch. His definitely held the most risk, at least at first. It was possible Karen could go in and out of the country as a tourist and not be connected with Orgutsov's disappearance at all. He hoped that was the case, and tried to convince himself it would be. He wanted to get his mind clear of the whole matter before he got home to his family. He needed to spend some time with them tonight.

Susan had fixed spaghetti for supper, knowing it was one of Alex's favorite meals. He felt like he hadn't really been home in weeks. It was obvious the family felt the same way—they treated him like a guest, waiting on him hand and foot. The meal was full of talk and fun. That night in bed, Susan was very quiet. Alex knew she must be hurting, and she had to have a hundred questions. He reached out to hold her, but he could sense the reserve in her.

Susan was trying to think of the right questions to ask Alex. She knew if she pushed or said the wrong thing, Alex might become defensive and withdraw from her, but she couldn't stand not knowing what was going on. She felt she might have somehow been responsible for Alex's recent behavior, but she couldn't think of anything she had done. Finally, in an attempt to reach out, Susan asked Alex if there was something bothering him he would like to share with her. When Alex very quietly said, "No, why?" Susan pulled away, turned over and softly cried herself to sleep.

Alex had hoped to share a special time with Susan that night before becoming totally absorbed in the mission. What could have been a romantic night, instead became a night of tears, distance and emotional pain. He came close to telling her, wanting her to understand what was going on, but it was too dangerous. His heart was aching because of his love for her. To even imagine anything happening to Susan or the children was more than he could stand.

Alex had seen what happened to people who were involved in espionage and who got caught or found out. The KGB and similar agencies know getting an agent's family produces even better results than getting the agent himself. That was the main reason he had quit CAFI after he married Susan. He wasn't going to risk anything happening to her. Now here he was involved again.

What was the matter with him? Was he crazy? He lay awake a long time thinking about it—long after Susan had fallen asleep. The world was hurting, too, and this was something Alex could do to help ease the pain for those who had a terrible disease. As soon as he got back, he would be able to explain everything. "As soon as he got back." That was positive thinking. It sounded like he was just going on a vacation.

Alex continued to rationalize. If he got caught, J. L. would protect his family. If Susan didn't know anything, she wouldn't be worried and upset. He put his arms around Susan and drifted off to sleep, believing he was doing the right thing.

6

It was time for the first test. Alex flew the Eagle north to the Sheppard One Military Operational Area (MOA) near Wichita Falls. Just before entering the MOA, Alex contacted Sheppard Approach Control on the UHF radio.

"Sheppard Approach, this is DEW Test One with you at ten thousand feet requesting a radar position check."

"DEW Test One, Sheppard Approach, squawk code 6677 and come up discreet low altitude frequency please."

"DEW Test One, Roger."

The code Alex had been given was a transponder code which would be assigned to his aircraft and his aircraft only. It allowed the controller to positively identify Alex's plane. The discreet low altitude frequency was one that had been prearranged for the test so no other aircraft could monitor the radio transmissions.

If it went as Alex hoped it would, he would be getting some very strange position reports. The controller handling his flight had a top secret clearance and had been specifically selected to be part of today's test. Alex set the transponder code in the disponder, selected the correct radio frequency, and contacted the controller. "Sheppard, this is DEW One, squawking 6677."

"Roger, DEW One. I show you on the one-five-zero degree radial, seventy-three miles."

"Good, Sheppard. Standby."

The position the controller reported was Alex's exact position according to the Distance Measuring Equipment (DME) installed in the plane. He selected a displacement on the disponder, waited one minute, and then radioed Sheppard again."

"Sheppard, DEW One requesting position report."

"Roger, DEW One. I show the one-nine-five degree radial, six-zero miles." Alex smiled to himself. The airplane had moved less than three miles, yet the disponder caused it to appear on radar as if it were approximately sixty miles from its true location. The disponder worked! He tried another one. This time the radar position showed him north of Sheppard by fifty-five miles. That was over a hundred mile displacement. After a fourth test, Alex was ready to return to Dallas and give Bud the good news. The next flight test would test the multiple target function. They also had altitude readouts to test. Alex had not expected the first test to go as well as it did, though Bud had been confident. So confident, in fact, he had declined to go along on the test. He said he preferred to spend his time working on the next phase of the project.

Three days later, Alex was in the Eagle again. This time Bud was with him. They planned to give the radar controller quite a show. After several position changes, they tried the multiple target function. The controller said he saw three targets, even though Bud had set the disponder to show six. The second test brought the same kind of results. The third didn't work at all. Disappointed, the two men headed back to Dallas.

After landing at Addison and putting the Eagle in the hangar, Bud pulled the disponder out of the plane and took it back to his shop. Alex checked his messages, then drove over to Karen's office.

Karen was just finishing up her office visits for the day and was headed to the hospital to check on a patient scheduled to undergo surgery the following morning. She told Alex, "If we had Dr. Orgutsov's cure, my patient wouldn't need the extensive surgery she will be having tomorrow. As it is, I might be able to buy her a year, maybe two, and they will be uncomfortable years. With his cure, we could free her from that cancer for good." There was such conviction in her voice, Alex felt it too. Karen obviously believed in what they were doing and that supported Alex's own conviction.

"What's the deal with your tourist visa?" Alex asked.

"I may have to go to Washington to the Russian Consulate to pick it up in person," she told him.

"Won't that arouse suspicion?"

"I don't know, Alex. I hope not. It would help me to visit the Intourist office in Washington to confirm my train and hotel reservations. Since I've been in the country before, they might just rubber stamp everything."

"On the other hand, they might consider you a threat to their newly-imposed restrictions."

"It's funny," Karen observed, "they don't want anybody to believe there are any restrictions."

"Yeah, but when you went before, you went for religious reasons. I don't think they're so open to that anymore."

Karen laughed. "They'll never be able to stop what was begun during the days of Yeltsin and their attempts at democracy. The people were crying out for spiritual renewal and they got it. Everybody, except the leaders, that is."

"Yeah," Alex added, "and they are the leaders who are now in power and who feel the most threatened by the influences of Christianity, Democracy and Capitalism."

"But they can't admit it," Karen pointed out.

"They can't admit it," Alex agreed.

"So, I'll go get my visa and everything will hopefully go forward as planned."

"I hope you're right. When will you go?"

"Day after tomorrow."

"Good. First, we need to get together tomorrow night and reconfirm your itinerary. Then we've got to start teaching you some Russian. We've got about three weeks. During that time,

I want you to learn enough of the language to get you across the country and out of a bind if need be. We can start on that tomorrow night as well. Then we will need to drill you some every day until it's time for you to go. I've got a lot of work to do myself, so we'll be busy. What's your patient load like?"

"Pretty heavy, but I am arranging to shift some of it over to Dr. Nelson. He'll take care of things while I'm gone, but I have several operations that cannot wait until I get back. I'll need to schedule those."

"That's all right, we'll need to do most of our work at night. Susan's not going to like it, but I don't see how we have any other choice."

"I know she trusts you, Alex. You don't have anything to worry about."

"I know, Karen, but there has been such a strain on our relationship lately because I haven't told her what I've been doing and I can't tell her what we are planning to do. These next few weeks aren't going to help that."

"Don't worry about it," Karen told him.

He looked at her questioningly.

"It will be all right," she affirmed.

The testing of the disponder continued, with the results getting better every day. Karen obtained her visa and made her travel arrangements. She and Alex spent every hour together they could, often until the early morning hours, going over the plan and studying the language.

During the day, when he was not flying the Eagle, Alex took care of other details that needed to be done. He made one trip to Alaska via the airlines, but did not tell Karen the purpose of the trip.

As the time for Karen to leave grew nearer, Alex spent more and more time going over the country's geography with her and drilling her on the language. He was confident in her abilities, but he still felt uneasy about her going.

At home, Susan was becoming distant. A wall was being erected between them and the fact Alex could not talk about what he was doing, didn't help. He didn't tell Susan he was with Karen every night, nevertheless she knew they were spending a lot of time together. Alex wondered if maybe that was what was bothering Susan. Maybe Susan resented the fact Alex was not always as open with her as he was with Karen. What could he say to her to dispel any doubts or fears she might have? How could he explain, without telling her the whole story? He couldn't. He'd just have to make it up to her when he got back.

Finally, on May 13, Karen left for what Susan thought was a European vacation. Thinking she would finally get some time with Alex, Susan was relieved to see Karen go. Two days later, Alex announced he was going to Alaska for a few days and he would be flying up there in the Eagle. Susan was crushed. Alex just stood and looked at her as she cried, but there was nothing he could say to comfort her. He tried to hold her in his arms, but she was reserved—as if she wanted to be comforted by him, but was unable to receive it.

7

Andy Young did the modifications to the Eagle as Alex had requested. The disponder was checking out fairly well on its test, although testing was not complete. As Alex left Dallas on the morning of May 16, he felt comfortable with the airplane and its ability to perform the mission. He wished he felt as comfortable with himself. He thought of Karen and the way she had applied herself to this mission. The hours they had spent together during the previous weeks rekindled some of the closeness they had experienced while growing up together. Each of them had depended upon the other for emotional support during the difficult times in their lives, although Alex had always felt like he depended upon Karen more than she upon him. If anything happened to her on this mission, Alex knew he would never forgive himself for letting her be involved.

Alex's initial flight plan called for a non-stop flight to Great Falls, Montana. Flight time would be a little over seven hours. He had topped off all of the Eagle's auxiliary tanks before leaving Addison Airport. This flight would give him a good chance to measure the actual fuel flow performance of the Windecker and help him determine what his absolute maximum range would be. The latter part of the flight, after he passed Denver, was over some spectacular scenery. From Great Falls, Alex would fly to Calgary, Alberta. The next morning he would fly to Fort St. John in British Columbia where he would pick up the Alaska Highway and follow it to Fairbanks.

Alex took one suitcase with various items of clothing he knew he would need and a sleeping bag. He also took a survival kit containing many items which might prove useful if he was forced down over some of the wilderness country he would be flying over. An autopilot had not yet been installed in the Eagle, yet Alex was able to trim the plane so it flew practically hands-off. The morning part of the flight was monotonous, but by early afternoon Alex began enjoying the awe-inspiring scenery as he flew over portions of the Rocky Mountains.

Landing at Great Falls, Alex had the fuel tanks topped off. The flight had taken seven hours and twenty minutes and the plane had burned one hundred and two gallons of fuel. That figured out to just under fourteen gallons an hour with an average groundspeed of one hundred and fifty knots. Alex was pleased.

Meanwhile, Karen arrived in Moscow on an Aeroflot flight from Paris. She checked into the National Hotel on October Square. Her room was on the fourth floor with a window overlooking the square below. The trip had been tiring, so she slept a few hours before going downstairs to the hotel dining room for dinner. Karen knew her presence in the Soviet Union as an American woman traveling alone would naturally arouse some suspicion. Traveling with a tour group would have been ideal, but they had not had enough time to coordinate that. Besides, if she started traveling with a tour group, then later split off from them as she tried to make contact with Dr. Orgutsov, she would arouse more suspicion. It was important, then, for her to act like a tourist in case she was being watched. Karen had two days to spend in Moscow before she would begin traveling east via rail.

That evening, she dined in the hotel dining room, then visited the Intourist desk in the hotel lobby. The clerk spoke English. Karen asked for recommendations for two days worth of sightseeing in and around Moscow, and confirmed the travel itinerary for her trip east. The Intourist clerk was helpful and friendly. She explained to Karen the importance of sticking to her planned travel itinerary or reporting any changes to an Intourist office within 48 hours. Karen had been given a brochure by the Intourist Bureau in Washington listing the places throughout the fifteen provinces of the Soviet Union for which travel permission is easily obtained. She must stay overnight in each town listed on her itinerary as an overnight stop, presenting her passport and travel visa at the hotel desk. Of course, she and Alex had gone over all of these rules before, but it reminded Karen of how careful she would have to be to keep from drawing unnecessary attention to herself.

Karen spent her second day in Moscow seeing the Kremlin, the Armory Museum, the Historical Museum, Assumption Cathedral, the Manege and other places of interest. The 13th–17th Century suits of armor, the early weapons and the art exhibits were fascinating. She thought of Alex when she saw the Manege and wondered if he had ever seen it. She decided he probably had and knew he would have been intrigued by its engineering. Being somewhat of a history buff, Karen wished she could spend more time in the museums. She wanted to keep moving, however, so she could better determine if she was being watched.

On her second day in Moscow, she visited G.U.M., the government department store and bought some clothing that would be appropriate for cross-country travel. In the afternoon, she visited Basil's Cathedral, and walked through Red Square and Sverdlov Square. She dined that evening in the Moscow Hotel and attended a concert at the Bolshoi Theater.

Several blocks northeast of the hotel in which Karen was staying, Colonel Veektor Zhukov of the new KGB was being informed of Karen's activities. He was in his office with an agent who had been mildly curious about the American doctor's presence in the Soviet Union alone, and for the second time in just a few weeks. The agent had monitored Karen's activities for the past two days and had found nothing unusual. Nevertheless, he and the Colonel were still interested in finding out the true purpose of her visit if she wasn't there to sightsee.

"Comrade Colonel Zhukov, Dr. Karen Webster is scheduled to depart Moscow via train tomorrow morning for a trip through the eastern provinces of the Soviet Union. We have no idea if she is truly on a sightseeing trip, or if she is an agent of the imperialist government sent here to steal secrets from the Soviet government. Shall I have her followed?"

"No, Comrade, we have her travel itinerary and can monitor her in each city in which she stops. We have no background information on this American physician, no record to indicate she has ever been suspected by the KGB of any espionage activities. Nevertheless, there is something about her name that is vaguely familiar to me. It is as if I have run across her somewhere in one of my own investigations, but merely as an incidental acquaintance of someone else in whom I was interested. It was many years ago, and I cannot remember the connection. Obviously he must have dropped from the scene, or I would remember. Perhaps it will come back to me."

"Yes, sir," the agent replied. "Dr. Webster has apparently visited our country before as a Christian missionary."

"Really?" Zhukov replied. "I find that interesting. Are you sure she's not on any of the lists of mission activists who we are to guard against?"

"She didn't show up on any of those lists. She must not have any ministerial credentials."

"That's fine. We have plenty of time to determine if she is up to no good. She will be on that train for many days before she leaves our country. And she will have to come back from the east and we will intercept her and if she has done anything illegal in our country, we will find out and deal with her then. Perhaps she is just as she said, 'fascinated by the history and geography of our beautiful country.'"

"Perhaps so, Comrade Colonel. Nevertheless, I must say I am very suspicious."

"She is just a woman, Comrade, and a novice at that. How much damage can she do?" said the Colonel.

"I would still like to have your permission to have the KGB at Sverdlovsk monitor her activities there."

"Very well, but do not get too carried away. If she has any real purpose here, it must be much further east. Why else would she go to such godforsaken places as some of the villages in eastern Siberia which she intends to visit?"

The agent departed, leaving Colonel Zhukov to wonder from where in his past he had encountered the name of Karen Webster, M.D., an American woman he was certain was not a spy. The Colonel walked over to his window and looked out upon Dzerzhinsky Square. He gazed at the statue of Dzerzhinsky, who had been the first head of the Soviet Security forces. Help me to remember, old man, he thought. If this American doctor's presence here is important, I must find out. There are rumblings afoot about replacing me.

On the morning Karen got on the train, she knew she had at least four days travel ahead of her before there was even a chance of meeting up with Dr. Orgutsov. He was spending several days at each town on his itinerary; Karen was spending one day at most. She and Alex had carefully worked out a plan to intercept the Russian doctor somewhere between Krasnojarsk and Jakutsk. If everything went according to plan, Alex would meet them in Jakutsk. Karen was nervous, but not overly so. The danger would come several days from now. She planned to spend the next few days enjoying the sights, yet she couldn't help but think about Alex and what he would be going through to get to her. He had purposely kept from her the details of how he planned to get to the rendezvous site. He didn't want her to worry or be responsible for the knowledge in case something went wrong. But Karen knew some of the logistics that had to be accomplished and she knew Alex would be exposing himself to a lot of danger, both on his flight into the country and during his time on the ground coming to meet her.

Karen found her place in a two-berth compartment or "kupeiny" and sat down. She wondered who she would share the compartment with and if it would be possible to carry on any conversation. Alex had drilled her on the basic phrases she would need to get by and she had done pretty well in Moscow. She hoped to get someone who would be patient and would work with her as she attempted to improve her skill in the Russian language. But, when the train finally moved out, Karen was alone in her compartment.

8

Alex called Susan from the hotel in Calgary. He wanted so much to explain to her what he was doing, but he didn't dare. She would probably think he was having some kind of mid-life crisis and was off doing something stupid. At first their conversation was subdued and strained. Finally, Alex said, "Susan, please trust me. I am involved in something very important. For security reasons, I can't tell you or anyone else about it. Please, it has to be this way. I don't want this to affect our marriage any more than you do."

"Alex, even Bud doesn't know what you're doing. And he's pretty upset about you taking that plane away while he was testing that gadget of his."

"I know, Susan, but I'll have it back to him soon. Besides, it's through testing and ready to go into production."

"Yeah, Alex, but Bud says you have the prototype and he's furious. There are apparently some changes in that box that haven't been documented in the engineering drawings yet."

"I know he's mad, but he'll get over it. This is extremely important, Susan."

"But where are you going?"

"I can't tell you, sweetheart. Let's just say 'Alaska'."

"Alex, is Karen with you?"

"Karen went to Europe. You know that."

"Okay, Alex, but please be careful," Susan finished. Alex heard reservation in her voice. He wanted to reach through the phone lines to touch her, to hold her, to reassure her, but he couldn't, so he just told her he loved her and hung up.

The following morning, Alex departed Calgary for Fort St. John, British Columbia. He landed at the Fort St. John Airport and picked up some charts for the trip up the Alaska Highway to Fairbanks. He also purchased a complete set of aeronautical charts for all of Alaska, which included the easternmost part of the Soviet Union. Departing the Fort St. John Airport, Alex picked up the highway west of town. He followed the highway to Fort Nelson, then on to Liard River. Three hours after leaving Fort St. John, Alex was over Watson Lake. He decided to continue on to Whitehorse in the Yukon Territory. He stopped at Yukon to stretch his legs and get something to eat. An hour later, he was back in the air for the two and a half hour flight to Fairbanks.

Alex was bone tired when he hit the bed in the hotel room in Fairbanks. Even so, he didn't go to sleep right away. He tried to imagine Karen on the train, alone in a country totally unfamiliar to her and potentially hostile to her if anyone suspected her real purpose in being there. He also tried to imagine Susan back in Dallas, having her husband off on some mysterious trip in which she had no idea where he was, when he was coming back or who he might be with. He also thought of the job ahead of him.

Flying the Eagle into Russia wasn't going to be the hard part. The most difficult part of the mission would start once he was on the ground in that country and had to hide the plane, find a way to refuel it for the flight home, find Karen and Dr. Orgutsov, and get back to the plane undetected. There were certainly a lot of variables affecting the risks he would be taking. If he were caught before meeting up with Karen and the doctor, it would only be his life at stake. Once they were with him, he would be responsible for all three of their lives. It was hard to sleep with such an awesome undertaking ahead. Once again Alex tried to figure out why he was doing it. Was it CAFI's subliminal coercion or something else? Was it simply because Karen had wanted him to? Pondering that thought, Alex drifted off to sleep without coming up with an answer.

Alex awakened early to prepare for the flight to Nome. It was approximately 500 miles over rough terrain and the weather left a lot to be desired. Alex had the plane fueled, filling the entire 215 gallon capacity tanks Andy had managed to get into the plane's wings and fuselage. Fuel at Nome was more expensive and Alex would just have to replenish the amount he burned on his flight from Fairbanks. He checked the weather and was relieved to find he did not have to file an instrument flight plan. Alex did not want to leave any record of his route of flight if he didn't have to. He risked traveling over some very rough terrain in Alaska with no one primed to look for him if he had to make a forced landing somewhere. That was just a chance he would have to take. The engine on the Eagle had been carefully examined by Andy Young before Alex had begun flying the plane. He had confidence in the mechanical condition of both the engine and the composite airframe.

Late that afternoon in Nome, Alex taxied to a brown metal building at the far south end of the airport. Parking in front of the hangar door, he got out of the plane and went in. He was expected. Alex had flown to Nome a few weeks earlier on Alaska Airlines and made the arrangements for what now needed to be done. The hangar door was opened and the Eagle towed inside. Alex borrowed an airport jeep and went to town to find a hotel room for the night. He spent the evening going over maps and aviation charts as well as some of the intelligence information he had picked up in New Orleans. He carefully plotted his course on the charts and figured fuel and groundspeeds. Since he would not have accurate weather forecasts for the portion of his flight inside the Soviet Union, he would have to allow extra margins in his planning. Alex had a suitcase full of clothing and other items he might need. He checked over those items, trying to think if there was anything he had missed.

The work on the plane was to take two days, so Alex slept late the following morning. He had an early lunch at the hotel and afterwards, took a walk. He did his best thinking while walking, and in his head he carefully went over the many details of his plan. So much of what happened once he was in the Soviet Union would have to depend upon his ability to improvise. It had been ten years or more since he had been in the country and so much there had changed. From what he could determine, during the period of openness there had been a mixed reaction to the presence of Americans in the various Sovet countries. Some had welcomed the Americans and their ideas of freedom. Others had turned against the greed and depravity capitalism had brought to their land. He had no idea what kind of support he could muster from local citizens, if needed. They might support him; they might turn him over to the government. Since there were so many unknowns, he had to make sure the parts of the mission he could control went without a hitch.

Karen would be in Krasnojarsk in three days. From that point her search for Orgutsov would be critical. He hoped the KGB was not onto her. If they suspected anything, the mission would be in jeopardy due to her inexperience. Alex had coached Karen on how to watch for them, hoping she would be able to recognize a tail if she picked one up. He had provided her with some excellent methods of escaping them, but hoped she would not have to use them.

He thought about Orgutsov. Did the doctor really expect Karen to arrange his defection? Would he be watching for her? Would he really defect, or would he expose them to the authorities? Despite so many unknowns, Alex remained calm. Amazingly, his only worry was for Karen. He had slipped back into the self-assured, calm, collected personality that had made him a CAFI candidate. He only hoped he still had the quick-thinking-under-pressure skills that had kept him out of trouble in those years when he had been active as a spy.

The following afternoon, Alex went to the airport to check on the Eagle's progress. The door to the hangar was locked. Alex knocked and waited to be let in. When he entered, he saw the Eagle's former royal blue color had been changed to a dark olive drab. The paint job cost him three thousand dollars cash, no questions asked. He and Karen had pooled together the money for this mission from their respective savings. For Alex, it was a sacrifice. He had been saving to buy some land so he and Susan could build a house in the country. She would be really upset if she knew how he was spending their money. Karen was a little better off, yet even she did not have money to throw away. In a way, Alex hoped it was CAFI's mission. Then they could pay the bills.

Alex paid for the paint job and paid to have the plane topped off. He had the fuel truck brought to the hangar so the plane could stay inside until it was time to depart. Joe Ferrell, the mechanic who had painted the plane, commented, "Mister, I don't know where you're going in that plane and I don't want to know. I just hope you're not planning on flying any dope, because I don't hold with that kind of stuff." Alex assured him he wasn't. Joe wanted to paint the FAA registration numbers back on the plane, but Alex told him he would take care of that later. Joe did not like it. He was an honest man, but he needed the money and Alex had paid him well. He was just glad he had not been asked to sign his name to the aircraft logbook to indicate he had painted the plane.

From this point on, timing was very critical to Alex. He had to fly under cover of darkness, yet had to plan his landing for first light. He would not be able to land in the darkness, yet he wanted to get on the ground and get the airplane under cover before there were people stirring about. Navigating over the water and the sparsely populated terrain of the eastern Soviet Union in the dark was going to be challenging. Alex was psyching himself up for the mission. He borrowed the jeep again and drove into town to buy food for the trip.

Returning to the airport, he waited for Joe to go home for the night before making final preparations for the trip. As soon as he was alone in the hangar, he dug a template out of his briefcase. It was a star—the type found on Soviet military aircraft. He took a can of red spray paint and painted four stars on the airplane, one on each wing and one on each side of the tail. There were virtually no civil aircraft in the Soviet Union except for commercial carriers. He did not intend for the Eagle to be seen, but if it was, he hoped whoever saw it would be ignorant enough of military aircraft to be fooled. Even those in the military would not know for sure whether or not their government had some new kind of experimental plane. Alex had learned from his previous experiences in Russia he could play their fears to his advantage. The average Russian, civilian or military, was generally afraid to question what he or she did not understand. A person acting with confidence and boldness could get away with a lot in that type of environment.

Alex estimated his flight time for the fourteen hundred and fifty mile trip at nine hours and ten minutes. When the time was right, he rolled the Eagle out of the hangar, climbed in and took off. His destination: Magadan in eastern Siberia!

9

The first few hours of Karen's train voyage gave her an opportunity to grow accustomed to her surroundings. The fact she was traveling first class did not isolate her from passenger contact. Travel in the Soviet Union is relatively cheap and many of the first class passengers were Soviet citizens on a holiday or on a journey to visit relatives. The passengers in the compartments surrounding Karen's were at first content to gaze at the scenery, to sleep or to talk among themselves. The first time she asked one of them a question, the news spread fast that she was an American. At once, the curiosity of her fellow travelers overcame any reserve they might have had. Many of them had never seen or talked to an American, much less had the opportunity to converse at length. The language barrier did present a problem, at least at first. Alex's lessons helped, plus the fact Karen carried a Russian pocket dictionary. She found the Russians very helpful in coaching her in her attempts at finding the correct pronunciation and in helping her to learn new words. When it came time to eat or whenever she had other needs, they saw to it she was taken care of.

One lady who said she had relatives in the United States knew a little English and she moved from her compartment to share Karen's two-person compartment. That was somewhat of a relief to Karen, for she wasn't sure how the sleeping arrangements would work for the nights she would spend on the train. What she noticed was even though the berths were not segregated between men and women, the sexes generally rearranged themselves that way for convenience. Karen's new friend, Anna, not only enjoyed trading language lessons with Karen, she pointed out interesting sights along the way. Karen hoped they would be traveling together for much of her journey. Since Anna was traveling as far as Novosibirsk, there was a good chance they would continue to enjoy one another's company.

Late in the afternoon, Anna began to doze and Karen found herself being lulled by the steady sound of the train wheels on the rails. She closed her eyes, but couldn't sleep for thinking of Alex. What had she gotten him into? Was all of this just a crazy notion of hers? Was she asking him to risk his life on something that might not even be real? No, she was certain of Orgutsov and his sincerity. The end of suffering his cure could bring was worth the risk to her, but what about Alex? Was she justified in asking him to risk his life for something *she* believed in? Had he done it just for her, or because he believed in it too? Karen couldn't be sure. He was the one being exposed to all of the danger.

Karen could pass herself off as a tourist, even after Alex and Orgutsov were together. She had entered the country legally and could leave legally, but Alex was a different story. He could be shot for what he was doing. If they caught him and could in any way tie him to his background, he most certainly would be treated as a spy.

Karen tried to visualize where Alex was now—somewhere in Alaska, she supposed, preparing for a very dangerous flight into the unknown. She should have talked him into letting her come with him. He shouldn't be alone on such a journey. But that wasn't the best plan. Alex knew it and Karen became convinced of it too. The uneasiness of worrying about Alex made Karen restless. She got up to go to the restaurant car. Anna awoke at Karen's movement and decided to go with her. Karen appreciated the company. She didn't need to spend too much time alone these next few days.

10

Colonel Zhukov could not sleep. His was an extremely difficult job. When the Democratic extremists allowed the old Soviet Union to collapse, they had opened the doors of the Union to anyone who wanted to come in. The mother country had been exposed to myriads of outsiders who had come in to exploit and proselytize her people, and to steal her resources. Now that the new government had realized the error of its ways and had given the revitalized KGB the charter to guard the Soviet Union's heritage, the task of doing so was almost impossible. Yet, he was expected to do the impossible.

Parliament was its own worst enemy. While attempting to regain control of the people, they had simply refused to recognize the fact that the only way to eliminate the influence of outsiders was to totally shut them off; to refuse them entrance into the country.

It was greed which prevented them from doing so. Many members of parliament were among those who had engaged in enterprises with the capitalists. Now they wanted the best of both worlds—a tightly controlled society that could be depended upon to do the predictable, and the financial rewards that came with the freedom to do the unpredictable. If it were not so frightening, the Colonel would have found it quite amusing.

Tonight it was the female American doctor who stirred his ulcer. He was puzzled about her. Karen Webster was not known to Zhukov, yet her name was somehow familiar. An American woman traveling alone was rare, though not unheard of. The fact she had been to the Soviet Union twice this spring was a bit unusual, yet the first time had been business. This trip appeared to be nothing more than a sight-seeing trip by a tourist who had been curious and had no time to satisfy any of that curiosity on her previous trip. Yet the fact she had spent only a couple of days in Moscow, no time in Leningrad, and was now heading for some of the more isolated spots of eastern Asia was unusual. What was there to draw her to the eastern cities when she had seen so little of Soviet Europe and Western Asia? Could it be she was simply a church activist, sent by the American church to stir up the proselytes they had managed to dupe into following their religion? If so, he didn't consider her particularly dangerous. Most of the Christian movements across the country had seemed to dissipate as the American influence upon them dwindled. But if she was there for political reasons, he had better find out the purpose of her visit.

He was awake most of the night trying to remember why her name seemed so familiar. He had requested a routine check on her through his contacts in Washington, but it would be at least 24 hours, perhaps longer, before they got back to him. Meanwhile, she was moving steadily across the continent.

During the early morning hours it came to him as a ghost from his long ago past—Karen Webster had been a friend of his one-time arch rival, the American agent Alex Davis! Davis had been one of the most successful infiltrators of the Soviet military system Zhukov had ever confronted. The fact Davis had blatantly flaunted himself in front of Zhukov on numerous occasions while impersonating a Soviet Air Force Major had been nothing less than a defiant slap in the face. Zhukov had hated the American, yet could find no one among his superiors who believed him when he told them Major Kotosvk had defected and was being impersonated by an American. They had practically laughed at him and humored him while asking to see his proof. At one time they had even interviewed Davis, posing as his Soviet counterpart, and he had fooled them. That had made Zhukov even more angry.

Finally, he had devised a plan on his own that had resulted in Davis being killed. It had cost the Soviet Union one of their MIG 23s, but that was a small enough cost to pay for ending the spy's stealing of State secrets. Davis had been killed ten years earlier, so what was Karen Webster doing in the Soviet Union now? How close had they been? Had she known about

Davis' undercover life? Those questions remained unanswered in Zhukov's mind.

He got out of bed and paced the floor, leaving his wife still sleeping in the bed. Perhaps the information he had requested from Washington would reveal a clue. Zhukov went into his sitting room and sat in a chair by the window overlooking the street below. He opened the blinds and peered outside at the darkness. His career had advanced significantly once the KGB had regained its former power, but not nearly as much as it would have, had he received the credit that should have been his for terminating the threat of such an illusive spy as Alex Davis. To this day, only he knew what he had done and how important it had been for the Soviet Union. Now he needed a known victory to his credit. It was time for him to pull off a major event or be passed over for the coveted post of Director of Security. Was this Dr. Webster thing something worthy of his attention, or should he let it pass by? Somehow his instincts told him he should pursue it. By tonight, he would know for sure. He was glad he had changed his mind and given permission to have the American followed.

Karen and Anna got off the train at Sverdlovsk. Karen had arranged for an overnight stay at the Intourist Hotel. Anna was able to change her travel plans so she could stay the night as well. The two of them spent the afternoon visiting shops and museums along the town square. Karen was grateful for the company and apparently Anna was as well. The two women hit it off quite well and Karen sensed the beginning of what could have become a close friendship had their lives not been so separated by geography. Each was getting better at the other's language. They laughed and joked at one another's clumsiness with certain phrases, but that made the learning all the more fun.

Anna seemed pleased at Karen's interest in her country. She appeared to enjoy the role of teacher and guide. That night instead of eating at the hotel restaurant, Anna called around and found them a highly recommended restaurant on the town square. Karen was content to let Anna do the ordering and she started with shchee, a cabbage soup with stewed beef in it. For the main course, Anna ordered bef-Stroganoff and some piroshkee, the latter being something like a doughnut filled with chopped meat. Along with the meal, they had a native wine, a sweet Madeira that came from the Crimea. There was music from a live band in the background. Karen really enjoyed the evening. It was not until later, when she was back in her room, that Karen allowed herself to think about Alex and his crossing of the Bering Strait alone at night in a single-engine aircraft that was on nobody's flight plan.

The next morning, the two women boarded the train again and settled into their compartment. At the end of this day, Anna would be getting off the train at Novosibirsk, while Karen would travel through the night to Krasnojarsk. She would have her first chance of meeting up with Dr. Orgutsov at Krasnojarsk. Where he would be in the town, she had no idea, but she would at least check the hospitals. She only wished Anna would be traveling further. The woman's knowledge of the language and customs would certainly prove valuable. Karen wondered how she could make inquiries without raising any suspicion. She hoped by presenting herself as a doctor, the local authorities would attribute her inquisitiveness to professional curiosity.

11

The water below Alex was filled with chunks of ice. He
had elected to fly west out of Nome instead of turning up the
coastline to Wales before crossing the strait. What difference
did it make if he crossed forty miles of sea or a hundred? He
was in forbidden territory anyway. He read the note on the
FAA chart, "FAA urges all pilots operating in the Bering
Strait area to take utmost precaution to avoid USSR airspace."
It meant nothing to him now. Alex would hit landfall in the
Soviet Union near the fishing village of Provideniya. That
would occur within an hour of his departure from Nome.
Long before that, Alex would be able to confirm whether or
not the Eagle really was invisible to Russian radar. His altitude
was 5000 feet. If the Eagle truly was radar invisible, there was
no advantage to flying low. At 5000 feet, the sound of his
engine would not attract attention from the villages along the
Russian coast.

Flying along with his lights off, forty-five minutes out, Alex
grew tense. He was watching for the MIGs that might be
coming any minute. Fifteen minutes passed with no sign of

126

interceptors. Below him, the Russian coastline became visible. The village lights indicated how sparsely populated the area was, yet Alex knew the coastline was well defended with squadrons of interceptors as well as surface-to-air missiles. He flew on, apparently unnoticed. After crossing the point of land that contained the village of Provideniya, Alex found himself once again over the icy ocean. Crossing the Gulf of Anadyr would put Alex out of reach of land for another hour and a half, yet to follow the coastline would cause him to burn more fuel and would expose him to an even greater chance of being sighted from the ground.

As the minutes passed and he found himself still alone in the sky, Alex began to relax. He had plenty of time to think and there was much to think about. The circumstances at his destination were unknown and it was still eleven hundred miles ahead. The engine droned steadily on, the gauges all indicating normally. Alex flipped the radio on and scanned the channels, listening for any sign the Soviets knew he was coming. The disponder remained off. The radio channels held only routine communications.

The problem of navigation was small for now. Alex could use the coastline and the Anadyr River for navigation the next couple of hours. After that, he would have a more difficult time. He would cross almost 500 miles of mountainous country before emerging again on the coastline near Manily. From there, he could more or less follow the coastline to

Magadan. Once he reached Magadan, his success would be determined by a combination of luck and skill. For a while, it would be mostly luck. Alex was going on knowledge that was ten years old, though it had been supplemented by some of the information he had gained from his visit to New Orleans.

The hours droned on and boredom became his companion. The novelty of flying the Windecker Eagle had worn off long ago, somewhere over Montana. The new Loran offered him a gadget to play with for a while, but navigation over the sparsely populated eastern Soviet Union offered few challenges and relatively few landmarks by which to check the Loran's accuracy. For a while he had listened to music being broadcast out of a station in Juneau, Alaska, but even that had faded out of range as the airplane flew westward away from North America.

Alex found himself fighting drowsiness in the early morning hours, and it renewed his admiration for Charles Lindbergh and his solo trip across the Atlantic in a single-engine plane a half a century earlier. He washed his face with water from the bottle he had brought along in the cockpit. He stretched his neck and moved around in his seat. An autopilot would have been welcome, yet Alex needed the concentration of flying to help him keep alert. He was now following the coastline of the Sea of Okhotsk and a new worry began to assail him—fog. There had been some clouds as Alex crossed the mountains, but he had been able to stay clear of them. Now wisps of fog were forming in the low-lying areas along the coast.

As daybreak approached, fog would become even more of a problem. Alex's timing was crucial. Landing in the broad daylight would surely attract attention he could not afford. Yet to land in the fog would be next to impossible. Alex had picked two possible landing sights, both in the Magadan area. One was an abandoned World War II airfield he was familiar with a few miles north of Magadan. The other was an aircraft graveyard further inland at Spurhoje. The abandoned airfield was his first choice. Hiding the plane there would be easier if the place was still as Alex remembered it. Fuel was not a problem in reaching either place. Alex would still have over three hours of fuel when he arrived. Daylight and fog *were* issues, however, and Alex was very concerned about both.

Magadan and daybreak arrived at the same time. There was fog in the low-lying areas, yet it lay close to the ground and Alex could make out man-made structures rising up through the fog. The area was very familiar to him, as he had flown into Magadan on numerous occasions in years past. Alex easily located the abandoned airfield and flew over it. He was aware of the sound of his airplane and how much attention it could attract, yet the runway, if it still existed, was not visible beneath the fog. Alex turned north, heading for Spurhoje and the dry lakebed which was the final resting place of outdated and worn-out Soviet military aircraft.

As he started to climb, he recognized a row of buildings that had once been military hangars. He reconstructed the layout of the land below from what he remembered. The runway, when it had been in use, had run north and south about 100 yards west of the row of hangars.

Alex had an idea. He positioned his airplane north of the old airport and began descending on a southerly heading. He aimed the nose of the Eagle at a point where he remembered the old runway to be and continued descending toward the fog. Alex had throttled the engine back, yet he kept his airspeed up, ready to abort the approach if he encountered any obstacles.

His biggest fear was of wires. Electrical power lines could destroy his airplane if he hit any at the speed he was traveling. The runway would probably be full of holes, yet the landing gear on the Windecker was tough. Alex continued his descent, straining forward in his seat looking for the ground. He entered the fog and kept descending, slightly shallowing his angle of descent. Suddenly, the wheels touched and he was down. The plane bounced once and Alex immediately closed the throttle and applied the brakes.

He was on pavement when he stopped, though it was old and cracked, with grass growing up through the cracks in the concrete. Alex cautiously taxied the plane toward the hangars. Visibility on the ground was very poor. Now the fog was an ally which would conceal his plane from anyone passing by. Alex kept the Eagle moving carefully, watching for obstacles or gaps in the pavement that might damage the plane. He arrived in front of a yellow metal building. Shutting the engine down,

Alex got out and approached the building which he recognized as an old military hangar. He pushed the door open slightly and discovered it was now being used to store wheat. Alex looked around for another building and found one two doors up that was only partially filled. He climbed back into the Eagle and taxied over to the half-empty building. He slid open the rusty hangar door and using a hand-held towbar from the Eagle's baggage compartment, pulled the airplane inside. He then closed the hangar door. Taking his suitcase and sleeping bag out of the plane, Alex crossed a grassy area about fifty feet wide behind the hangar and went into the woods. The sun was coming up and Alex knew the fog would soon lift. He was exhausted and all he wanted to do now was sleep, yet he had to remain awake for a while in case he had been seen or heard and someone came to investigate.

Alex found a place among the spruce trees on the side of a hill overlooking the airport. He spread out the sleeping bag and lay down, positioning himself so he could see the entrance to the hangar. As the fog lifted, Alex spotted several large tractors parked on what had been the runway. Fortunately they were clustered at one end and he had stopped before he reached them. Alex marveled at his luck. Impacting one of those tractors during his landing would have destroyed the Eagle and possibly Alex as well.

Now that he could see his surroundings, Alex understood why the hangars were full of wheat. The entire airport had been converted into wheat fields. Fortunately, the fields were already planted for the season and as Alex watched, there appeared to be no activity. He wondered where the farm headquarters was located, but that was something he could find out later. His pressing need at the moment was sleep.

Walking a short distance into the nearby woods, Alex found a small, concealed clearing and rolled out his sleeping bag. He crawled into it and slept for several hours. He woke up mid-afternoon and got up to look around. There was no sign of activity around the buildings or the tractors, but Alex knew he had to take steps to prevent the plane from being inadvertently discovered. He figured the best plan was an offensive one. He pulled a gray one-piece flight suit out of his suitcase and put it on. The shoulders of the flight suit contained the insignia of a Soviet Air Force Major. He wore a name tag which identified him as Major Alexi Korbut of the Soviet Air Force. He rolled up his sleeping bag, grabbed his suitcase and descended to the plane. Inside the hangar, he saw no sign that anyone had tampered with the Eagle. Putting his suitcase and sleeping bag in the plane's luggage compartment, he locked the door and went back outside. He knew the city lay to the south, but where was the headquarters for the farm?

Alex walked to where the tractors were parked. Leading away from the concrete was a well-worn dirt road over which the big tractors had obviously traveled many times. Hoping the road would lead him to the farm headquarters, he started walking. Half an hour later, he came upon a cluster of buildings. Several looked like storage sheds. The one closest to the road had a door and glass windows. Walking up to that building, Alex called out in Russian, "Hello! May I use the telephone?" From inside he heard a stirring, then a sound like a chair being scooted across the floor. A young man in his early twenties and dressed in heavy work clothes came to the door. As soon as he saw Alex in military clothing, his attitude was one of respect.

"Comrade Major, come in. What is it I can do for you?"

Alex explained to him he needed to use the telephone to call headquarters. Of course he would pay the charges. The young man invited him in and pointed into the next room where the telephone was located. Alex picked up the receiver and dialed a number. He waited a moment before he began speaking. The young man had remained in the other room, but was standing within earshot.

Alex shielded the phone with his body and held down the receiver button with his finger. He spoke into the phone loud enough for the man to hear. Alex explained to "headquarters" how he had to make a forced landing in the experimental plane and he had to secure it until repairs could be made and fuel transported in. He made a convincing argument to his superiors who apparently left the details of working out his problem up to him. The young man listening gathered the Major was receiving very little support from his command.

That wasn't unusual. He felt he received little support from his own superiors. Alex's conversation on the phone was designed to gain a sympathetic ally in the young man listening and it was working.

Alex finished his "conversation" and hung up the phone. Before turning around to face the young farmer, he took on an expression of disgust. As he walked into the next room, Alex reached into his pocket and pulled out a few roubles and started to hand them to his host. The young man shook his head. "It's a government phone anyway." He introduced himself. "I am Grant Sopin. Is there any way I can help you?"

Alex spread his hands, a gesture of exasperation. "What can you do? It appears I have gotten myself into a problem with no easy solution."

Sopin looked puzzled. He was a strong young man, eager to help and obviously not a typical collective farmer. "Surely there must be something we can do?"

Alex leaned against a table and explained his "problem." "I am a test pilot who has been evaluating a new training airplane. I convinced my superiors to let me take the plane on an extended trip to test its reliability and its fuel consumption. They gave in to me reluctantly, but they thought I was foolish to attempt such a feat. It appears they were right. They said the plane was not yet ready for such an extended flight. I unfortunately didn't agree."

"So what happened?" Sopin asked.

Alex shrugged his shoulders in frustration. "The airplane developed a problem, though it is only a minor one. I need to get it repaired and refueled in order to save face."

"We can do that, can we not?"

Alex acted surprised the young farmer would want to help him, although that was exactly the response he was trying to solicit. "It would be good if we could," he answered. "My superiors are trying to make me out to be a failure."

"I know what you mean. It is always that way, it seems," Grant observed.

"I need simply to hide the plane until I can get some parts to repair it. It is an experimental design and should not be revealed to the public."

"Hide it? Where is this airplane?"

"I made an emergency landing at the old airfield you're now using for planting and storing wheat. I hid the plane in one of the hangars."

Sopin looked outside and up the road toward the airfield as if just now comprehending what had happened. "You have the airplane here, in one of our storage sheds?"

Alex nodded.

"Can I see it?"

"Yes. But first I must obtain permission from the manager of this farm to leave it there for a few days."

"I am the only one on the farm at this time. The others will not be back until the spring harvest season, which is still a few weeks away."

"Then how would you like to be the one who will guard my valuable airplane?"

Grant nodded eagerly. "I would like that very much."

"How very fortunate. I will be able to rest more comfortably, knowing it is in such capable hands."

Grant seemed pleased at the Soviet Major's confidence.

"I must go locate the necessary parts and to purchase some fuel for my return journey."

"Afterwards, when your plane is repaired," Grant asked, "perhaps the Major can give me a ride?"

Alex smiled. "Of course you may have a ride, if you are willing to risk your life in an experimental airplane." Grant nodded, all smiles.

Alex was waiting for his luck to change. Things were going too well. His landing in the fog without damaging the plane, plus the fact no one had been around to see him hide the Eagle, had been a stroke of luck. The fact he had found an ally in the first person he met, one who would help him insure the plane would remain hidden, was almost too good to be true. Of course he had many other problems to overcome. He had to find a good grade of gasoline for the plane and either steal it or buy it without raising suspicion. He also had to get to Jakutsk and locate Karen and the Russian doctor. Jakutsk was nearly 800 miles away by road and Alex needed to travel the distance in less than two days. He wished he could fly the distance, but it was too risky.

He knew of no place closer to Jakutsk where he could safely hide the plane. As far as he could tell from the research he did before leaving the States, there was no regular train that made the trip from Magadan to Jakutsk. Alex would have to find a vehicle. He wondered if he could borrow one from the collective farm, but he would have to be gone at least four days, during which time Grant might grow suspicious. Besides, as he looked around, all he saw was an old stakebed truck which did not look like it could go the distance. Perhaps there was an Aeroflot flight he could take. He would have to get into town to find out.

Alex made arrangements to borrow a bicycle from Grant that he could ride into Magadan. But first he took the young man to see the plane to satisfy his curiosity. Fortunately, Grant did not notice the American-made instruments and radios in the cockpit. He seemed to be genuinely convinced the Eagle was an experimental training plane of the Soviet Air Force. Once Grant's curiosity was satisfied, the two men went back to the farm headquarters. After exchanging his flight suit for civilian traveling clothes, Alex pedaled off into town.

Magadan was a fairly good-sized city for this region, with more than 100,000 inhabitants. The city was a trade center for the coastal area, with fishing villages to the east and south and farm and mining villages to the north. As the American rode into town on the bicycle, he was hardly noticed, that being a common mode of travel in this region. Alex headed for the downtown area, looking for the Intourist office. As he pedaled along, he took note of the businesses around him. Magadan was the gateway to the gold fields and coal mines that lay inland in the Magadan Province. The city was a major seaport and the home of several industries that supported the mining operations surrounding the city. There were also fish canneries in the area near the waterfront. Alex was sure there would be air service, though it was possible Jakutsk would not be readily accessible from there. It had been a good idea to change clothing. Traveling as a military man, especially a pilot, would have attracted unnecessary attention in this part of the country. The test pilot story had been a good one for Grant, but it was inappropriate now.

Near the main part of the city, a good three miles inland from the coast, Alex found the Intourist Hotel. Inside was the travel office. There he encountered another stroke of luck, as if someone was orchestrating this whole deal. An Aeroflot flight the next morning was bound for Jakutsk. Presenting one of the fake sets of identification papers he had obtained in New Orleans, Alex purchased a ticket. He then rode the bicycle back to the farm to enlist Grant's help with the fuel issue.

Back at the farm, Alex explained to Grant he needed to fuel the airplane before taking off so he could return to his home base. Hoping the farmer would not know enough about aircraft to think it an unusual amount, Alex explained he would need about six hundred and twenty-five liters of high grade gasoline. The tractors on the farm used diesel fuel, so there was no gasoline storage on the farm. The only gasoline vehicle was the truck which had a seventy liter tank.

Alex asked about the possibility of using one of the diesel tanks, cleaning it out and transporting it to town in the back of the truck. Grant was agreeable, but he suggested they use some two hundred liter drums instead. Empty ones could be obtained quite reasonably in town. Alex agreed that was a good idea and the two men jumped in the truck and headed into the industrial district of the city. As they drove along, Alex asked the younger man where they could obtain vouchers for such a large amount of fuel. Would they be able to buy the fuel and pay cash, or would vouchers be required? Grant thought the fuel would have to be purchased by vouchers if they bought it all at the same place, but if they shopped around, they might be able to buy gasoline in several locations and pay cash. The problem was the octane rating. The Eagle's engine had been modified to run on automobile gas, nevertheless, Alex wanted the best grade he could get.

He wound up settling for a mixture. They were able to fill two of the two hundred liter drums with 96 octane fuel, for which they paid cash. They filled the third one with 87 octane fuel using a voucher that had been purchased by the farm.

Alex reimbursed Grant for the voucher so he could replace it later and not incur the wrath of his foreman.

Back at the hangar, the two men pumped the fuel into the Eagle's tanks using a hand pump from one of the tractors. It was hard work. Alex filtered the fuel through a chamois cloth he had brought along for that purpose. Running the engine on Soviet automobile gasoline was risky enough without the added risk of putting contaminated fuel into the tanks.

It took the men several hours to complete the refueling operation. They alternated working the pump. When they had finished, Alex offered to treat Grant to dinner in town. The younger man insisted he be allowed to treat Alex instead. His arrival had given Grant something to break up the monotony of staying on the farm alone with little to do. He enjoyed cooking, but had no one to cook for.

That evening Alex was treated to a meal of cured sturgeon—or osytotr—borshch and borodinsky. The latter was a dark, sweet bread with caraway seeds on top. The meal was delicious. They washed it down with vodka, Alex being careful not to refill his glass too often.

The fellowship was rich. The lonely farmer wanted to know about flying and about military life. He was also a very good source of information about local conditions, but Alex was unable to learn much from him about what he might encounter on his travel westward. Grant had scarcely left the mines and farms around the Magadan Province. He built a fire to ward off the chill of the evening and after awhile, Alex stretched out on the sofa in front of the fire and drifted off to sleep.

Early the next morning, Alex pedaled to town and boarded the flight to Jakutsk. The check of his travel papers was cursory and he aroused no suspicion at the airport. As soon as the Ilushin airliner lifted off, Alex leaned back in his seat and closed his eyes. He wanted to avoid conversation, so he feigned sleep. However, as he closed his eyes, his mind was alive with activity. Alex had anticipated he would have to find and win an ally to help him hide the plane, but he never expected someone as congenial and willing to help as Grant had been. Somehow Alex believed he could trust the man and the Eagle's presence would not be revealed.

The fact he had been able to buy fuel through the auspices of a collective farm was also a stroke of good fortune. Alex had expected to have to steal the fuel and that would have increased his chances of discovery. With things going so well on his end, he couldn't help but wonder about Karen. Was she on schedule? Had she aroused suspicion? He wondered if she had located the doctor yet? Probably not, it was a little too early. As the twin-engine turboprop droned along on its five-hour flight, Alex thought ahead to what he would do when he reached Jakutsk. The first thing was to find the hospital where Dr. Orgutsov would be visiting. He would have to find a way to ask questions without arousing suspicion. That should be no problem. Alex was beginning to feel confident he could play any role that was necessary.

12

Karen watched Anna get off the train at Novosibirsk, then settled back into her seat. The train would not be in the station but a few minutes, so she had decided not to follow the Russian woman off the train. Then on an impulse, she changed her mind. Anna's companionship during the past couple of days had done a lot to put Karen at ease and she wanted to somehow express her thanks, perhaps just a warm hug. She got out of her seat and walked toward the front door of the rail car.

As she stepped off the train onto the platform, she saw Anna standing a few feet away, her back to the train, talking to a man in his forties. He was tall, well built and dressed in a dark suit. He carried a briefcase in his left hand, and over his arm was draped a dark overcoat. Karen surmised he must be a friend or relative of Anna's who had come to meet the train. As Karen started toward them, Anna suddenly hurried off into the station without looking over her shoulder. Karen shrugged, disappointed she had missed the woman, but unwilling to take a chance on missing the train, she climbed back up the steps to the passenger car and went back to her compartment.

New passengers were boarding the train and finding their seats. Karen was surprised when the man Anna had been talking to entered her compartment. He smiled and introduced himself in English, "Dr. Webster, I am Dmitri Flerov. My cousin, Anna, has just informed me you are an American tourist traveling in our country and she asked me to introduce myself to you. It just so happens I hold tickets for a seat in this compartment and would consider it a pleasure if I might join you."

"Yes, Mr. Flerov, you may join me," replied Karen. Her first thought was one of relief, for it appeared Anna had sent someone to take her place and now she would once again have the benefit of English-speaking companionship on her journey. When she reached Krasnojarsk that might present a problem, but it should be fairly simple to excuse herself and separate company when the time came. This Mr. Flerov seemed a pleasant enough individual. He spoke English quite well, in fact much better than Anna had, and if he were Anna's cousin surely he could be trusted. Karen watched Flerov as he put his briefcase and overcoat in the overhead luggage rack and settled into the seat across from her. He was dressed as she supposed most businessmen in the Soviet Union would be dressed and except for his eyes, he was a rather handsome man.

Karen was a student of eyes and believed there was so much you could tell about an individual by looking into their eyes. She had often found this fact helpful, not only in her role as a physician, but as a person who truly cared about others. She was gifted at penetrating the outer shell of someone who was hurting emotionally and getting that person to open up to her. Flerov's eyes were cold and lifeless. They were not the eyes of a gentleman who would go out of his way to help a stranger simply because his cousin had asked him to. Karen knew she could be wrong—she had been before—but not often. Her first impression had changed and now she knew this man would bear watching.

As the train began to move, Karen stared out the window. Suddenly a thought occurred to her—Dmitri Flerov had just addressed her as "Doctor" Webster! Karen had never told Anna she was a doctor. In fact, she had been careful to avoid letting the Russian woman know she was a physician, simply as an extra precaution against having anyone tie her prematurely to Dr. Orgutsov. She knew now she must be very careful. It was possible this man was with the KGB and had been sent to watch her. In that case, Anna, too, could have been an agent. Karen was disappointed, but Alex had warned her how easily she could be fooled by professional agents.

Now that it appeared she was being watched, Karen began experiencing fear for the first time. But it was fear mixed with excitement. Alex had spent a lot of time with her during the last few weeks teaching her what to do. She was certain she could pull off whatever she needed to and found herself looking forward to the challenge. Alex had warned her about that, too. Knowing how much like him she was in certain areas, he had been relatively certain role-playing and suspense would be to her liking. Neither of them had ever been content with the type of dull routine living so many in this world settle for.

Karen looked over at Flerov and found herself smiling a knowing smile. "I'll get you, Mr. KGB," she thought. "You may be a tail, but you most certainly will underestimate the training and preparation I have had from someone who very successfully fooled you people on numerous occasions." To avoid conversation for a while, at least until she could go over in her mind what she could or could not safely say, Karen feigned sleep. She hated to be anti-social to a new acquaintance, but this one was one she could not trust and he would just have to live with it.

Karen was weary and now she felt uneasy. She fought against it, but a certain amount of fear was haunting her. Back in the States, she had been so sure of herself. During her planning sessions with Alex she felt confident, primarily because he always instilled confidence in her. He always had. Even when she was little, Alex had always encouraged her to do more, to be more, and made her believe she could do it. It was Alex who, indirectly, had encouraged Karen to go to medical school. Now she was thousands of miles from home, in a foreign land and on a mission that was directly opposed to the government of that potentially hostile land.

Alex would meet her, but he was so far away, if he had even made it into Russia at all! His chances of discovery were much greater than her's. She had been on this train for days and her rendezvous with Alex and Dr. Orgutsov was still over a thousand miles away. Russia seemed to be an endless expanse of land. The one person she had met who possibly could have been an ally was apparently a KGB agent. For some reason, the Soviet secret police were on to her, though they couldn't possibly know for sure why she was in the country—unless Alex had been caught! Surely that had not happened or they would have arrested her as well. Somehow Karen knew she had to maintain her cool and act as if nothing were wrong. When she got closer to the Soviet doctor, she could play one of the aces Alex had so carefully prepared for her. Meanwhile, she tried to sleep to pass the time.

13

Alex landed in Jakutsk a little after noon. He took a taxi from the airport to the Ministry of Health Hospital near the center of the city. Entering the building, he sought out the administrator's office. With confidence, Alex approached the outer door of the office and walked up to the young woman who sat at the desk. He spoke easily in Russian, asking her if the administrator was in and if so, would he be able to see him. The woman said the administrator was away from his desk but would be returning shortly and asked if she could be of any assistance.

"Perhaps you can," Alex answered, speaking the Russian language as if he were a native. "I am Dr. Khromchenko from the Academy of Medical Sciences in Moscow. While I was attending a medical convention in Khabarovsk, I received a communication which urged me to meet Dr. Lev Orgutsov in Jakutsk to travel with him back to Moscow. I have misplaced the letter, which contained the exact dates he was to be here. I hope I have not missed him."

"Oh, no," the young lady replied. "Dr. Orgutsov has not yet arrived here. His visit is scheduled for the day after tomorrow, when he is to arrive by train."

"Spaseebo, tovarisch," Alex thanked her and turned around to leave.

"Zhdat," she said, stopping him. "I am sure the administrator will want to see you. It is not often we have visitors from the Academy of Medical Sciences, and this week we are to be honored with two."

"Don't worry. I will return," Alex assured her, "to meet with Comrade Dr. Orgutsov when he arrives." Smiling, he walked down the corridor to the front door and out into the street.

He had almost blown it! Doctors from the Academy of Medical Sciences were well known throughout the medical profession and he had just used a made-up name, rather than a real one. If the administrator had been in, his cover might very well have been blown. It was obvious the visit of Dr. Orgutsov was being considered a special occasion. A second doctor from the famous institute, especially one arriving unannounced, was something Alex now realized was very much out of the ordinary. He hoped the woman would not make a big deal of it to her superior.

Alex now had two choices. He could wait in Jakutsk for Karen and Dr. Orgutsov to arrive, or he could travel westward to Krasnojarsk and hope to meet up with them there. He was leaning toward the latter choice because it would have him at least doing something. Waiting in Jakutsk for two days, not knowing how Karen was doing or where she was, did not appeal to him, even though it might have been the safest avenue. He decided to go to the Intourist office and check the train and airline schedules between the two places. To arrive at Krasnojarsk too late would cause Alex to miss them. Whether or not he went would depend on the timing.

When Alex learned he could take an afternoon flight that would put him in Krasnojarsk that evening, he decided to take it. This time when he traveled, he used a different identity drawn from the forged documents he had obtained in New Orleans. Once again, he did not arouse any unnecessary suspicion as he traveled about the country disguised as a Soviet citizen.

Krasnojarsk was an entirely different setting from the smaller towns Alex had been in during the previous two days. He was now almost 1100 miles from Jakutsk, almost 1900 miles from where the Eagle was hidden near Magadan. His travel had gone very well. He hoped Karen's had been as successful. With any luck, he might be able to make contact with her within the next few hours. That would be risky, for if she had come under surveillance, then Alex, too, might be discovered. For Orgutsov, Karen and Alex to travel together as far as Magadan would be too risky. Yet the earlier they made contact with the Soviet physician, the sooner they would know if their mission was a legitimate one or not. Risks aside, they had to know where Dr. Orgutsov stood before they got in any deeper.

Alex wasn't sure, because of the language barrier, how Karen would make contact with Orgutsov and explain to him what they had planned. That was another reason he felt he needed to be near her. By telephone, he checked the train schedules. The next arrival from the west would be mid-morning the next day. According to his calculations, Karen would either be on that train or the one arriving later the following evening. He did not believe she could be in Krasnojarsk already. However, Orgutsov's itinerary indicated he was probably already in the city. Needing some sleep before proceeding further, Alex took a taxi to a hotel near the medical district and obtained a room. He decided to eat in the hotel dining room before going upstairs for some sleep.

As he was eating, Alex thought over the problem of insuring he would not miss Karen and Dr. Orgutsov. Since a meeting with Karen at the train station would be risky, he decided his first task would be to locate Orgutsov. He hoped Karen would be able to find him as well, but knew her best bet was to locate him on the train as he left for Jakutsk. Since she knew the doctor by sight, she would be able to walk up and down the train cars until she found him. From there, she would have to play it by ear.

Alex rose early, after a good night's sleep in the old, but comfortable hotel. There was no phone in his room, so he went down to the hotel lobby and placed a call to the Ministry of Health. He identified himself to the man at the other end of the phone as Dr. Yuri Yaralov, a colleague of Dr. Lev Orgutsov. He needed to confer with Dr. Orgutsov on a medical matter and was hoping to reach him via telephone. After a brief delay, Alex was informed the doctor was lecturing that morning at the Medical Technical Institute and could probably be reached by phone there. After asking for the telephone number, Alex thanked the man and hung up. He then called the Medical Institute only to find Dr. Orgutsov had just started a lecture that was to last two hours. He was due to have lunch with a group of medical specialists, and in the afternoon was to take a tour of the institute. Alex knew then his best shot would be to join the luncheon or the tour.

He had breakfast, then took a taxi to the Krasnojarsk Medical Technical Institute which was located on the banks of the Yenisey River. He was dressed in a gray business suit, which he hoped would help him pass as an official of the Ministry of Health. He planned to use that as a cover to get close enough to Dr. Orgutsov to have a private conversation with him.

Arriving at the administration building of the institute, Alex made a few low-key inquiries of people he observed to be low enough in rank or position for him to impress with his business suit and confident manner. He was able to determine the location of both Orgutsov's lecture and the luncheon being held in his honor. He knew, from the reaction to his inquiries, it would not be wise to walk into one of those places unannounced or unattended. For that reason, he solicited an escort from the administrator's office. He was assigned a young medical student who considered it an honor to escort the official from Moscow around the campus.

Alex was actually beginning to enjoy the role-playing. He had been quite good at it years earlier, yet had been away from any serious role-playing for a long time. He was pleasantly surprised at how easily the skills had come back to him. Now he was playing the role of an official of the Ministry of Health who had some business with Dr. Orgutsov. His identity could easily be checked through official channels, in which case he would obviously be revealed as a phony, but Alex relied on the fact he was doing nothing to arouse suspicion to prevent anyone checking up on him. Dr. Orgutsov's reaction to his visit would be the supreme test. The doctor could easily blow the whistle on him, which would mean the end of the game. For his sake, and for Karen's, Alex prayed that would not happen.

The two men slipped into the back of the room where Orgutsov was lecturing the students. Alex listened carefully to the man's words, but nothing sounded familiar to him. He did not appear to mention anything about a cure for cancer.

Alex studied Lev Orgutsov's features from his location near the back of the classroom. The doctor appeared to be in his sixties. He was grayheaded, with slightly thick and unruly hair, and wore glasses. He was a small man, perhaps five feet eight inches tall and Alex guessed he weighed around a hundred and sixty pounds. He was wearing a gray pinstripe suit that was wrinkled, but of good material. As he talked, he was obviously enthusiastic about his subject matter and he seemed to have the attention and respect of his audience.

When the lecture was over, Alex and his student escort approached the physician as he was gathering up his notes. Alex asked the student to excuse them, saying he would like to have a few words with Dr. Orgutsov alone. As the student retreated to the corridor outside the classroom, Alex decided to be as straightforward as he could, yet at the same time keep some options open in case Karen had severely misread the Soviet doctor.

"Dr. Orgutsov," Alex spoke, thankful his language lessons with Karen had resulted in his Russian being as good as ever. "I have come to you from the United States because of your letter to Karen Webster, the American doctor."

The Russian doctor looked at Alex, making direct eye contact. At first he appeared to be suspicious, but as he stood there a long moment, studying Alex's eyes, he was apparently struggling within himself. Alex simply waited. The next move had to be Orgutsov's. Finally, the doctor spoke, "Would you say that again, please?"

"I am here because of the papers you gave Dr. Karen Webster, and because of her belief that you wanted us to come for you."

"Us?" the doctor questioned.

"Yes, she is here, too."

"Where is she? I must see her."

"I don't know exactly," Alex replied. "She is coming from the west by train. She should arrive here today and will most likely be looking for you as you leave by train tomorrow."

"What is it you want from me?" Orgutsov asked cautiously. Alex considered the possiblity of a trap. He maintained eye contact with the doctor and after several seconds decided it was not. The doctor was apparently wary of a trap himself and was being extremely careful. Alex understood and respected him for it.

"I think you had better discuss that with Dr. Webster," Alex answered. He had to play it safe as well.

"Perhaps you could join me for lunch, Comrade. Exactly who should I introduce you as?" Dr. Orgutsov smiled as he asked the question. Alex began to feel he was really going to like this man.

"I am Dr. Yuri Yaralov, your colleague from the Academy of Medical Sciences in Moscow."

Orgutsov smiled again. "Who are you really? Or do you want to wait to tell me?"

"I will let Karen Webster introduce us. Meanwhile, I think it would be best if I stayed with you until you have a chance to meet with her. Do you think my presence here will arouse suspicion?" Alex asked.

"I don't think so," Orgutsov replied. "I am an honored guest here and they will treat you with respect as long as they think you are with me. There will be no one to question your identity until this afternoon. There are men and women on the staff of this institute who are quite familiar with my work and most of the people I work with at the Academy. To some of them you might arouse suspicion."

"Very well," said Alex. "After lunch I will return to my hotel and wait. What are the chances of you meeting Karen's train this afternoon?"

"Very slim, I am afraid. I have commitments throughout the evening. Where are you staying?"

"At the Yenisey Inn," Alex replied, "not far from the train station."

"Good," said the doctor. "I will meet you in the lobby at nine in the morning. We will go to the train station together. Perhaps you can locate Dr. Webster this evening."

"I don't think so," responded Alex. "She does not know I am here, nor does she have enough command of your language to seek you out. She will most likely be on the train tomorrow morning looking for you."

"I certainly hope so, Dr. Yuri Yaralov, for we have some rather important matters to discuss. I do not mind telling you your presence here unsettles me, even though it is something I asked for, hoped for, even planned for. I do not imagine I shall sleep very well this night. Come, let us enjoy the lunch they have prepared for us in the cafeteria." The older man took Alex's arm and guided him toward the door.

14

Karen's train arrived at Krasnojarsk shortly after three in the afternoon. She went immediately to the Yenisey Inn and checked in at the Intourist desk in the lobby. Her room was on the third floor overlooking the river. Dmitri Flerov had tried on several occasions during the train trip to get Karen engaged in conversation, but had been disappointed each time. Karen, who was naturally prone toward conversation with strangers, had found it difficult not to talk with the man, but she had been afraid he might trip her into unwittingly giving away some facet of her plan.

Upon leaving the train, Flerov had offered to accompany her to her hotel. When she declined, he shrugged and walked off to find a taxi. Now Karen wondered if he had followed her from a distance, or if he had an associate watching her now. Partly due to curiosity, and partly from a sense of adventure, she decided to try one of the disguises Alex had helped her develop. Then she would have a look around.

In her hotel room, she unpacked the gray skirt and plain white blouse Alex had picked for her in Dallas. To wear over the blouse, she had a heavy, black, man's sweater. After laying out the clothes, which sharply contrasted with the stylish clothing Karen usually wore, she turned her attention to her hair. She wet her hair and brushed through it with brown hair color which covered all traces of blonde or silver. After working with her hair a while, the result was dark hair pulled back into a bun. She dressed in the plain clothing, then removed her contacts and put on a pair of heavy, black-rimmed glasses. Looking in the mirror, Karen was satisfied she looked different enough to pass all but the closest scrutiny. She had changed the appearance of her facial features slightly by removing most of her makeup. To complement the outfit she was wearing, Karen carried a small black satchel, which replaced her purse. Her shoes were black loafers, slightly worn at the heels.

Checking the hallway, Karen left her room. Satisfied no one saw her, she bypassed the elevator and went down the stairs to the lower level. The hotel dining room was beginning to serve the evening meal, cafeteria style. Karen went in and entered the serving line. She chose her food by pointing and took her tray to a table near the back wall. Soon after she was seated, Dmitri Flerov walked into the dining room and looked around. He looked right at Karen with no sign of recognition. Then he entered the serving line himself. Karen couldn't help smiling as she realized Flerov had been looking for her and had been fooled.

She quickly recomposed her facial expression before he looked back her way. Alex had warned Karen her laughing eyes would be the one thing that could give her away. She had a way of finding humor in almost anything and a trained agent would pick up that trait in a hurry. Flerov seated himself two tables away from where Karen was seated. The entire time he was eating, he kept his eye on the doorway, with fleeting glances around the room. Karen surmised he must have already found a way of checking her room and knew she wasn't in it. The only logical place for her to be was in the dining room or the hotel lobby. The shopping district was too far away and would be closed at this hour.

Karen finished her meal and walked out onto the hotel veranda overlooking the Yenisey River. The night air was cool, and she gathered her sweater about her. Dr. Orgutsov was somewhere in this town. She should be able to spot him in the morning as he boarded the train. His itinerary had indicated he would be on the first train out the next morning. Karen prayed that Alex was close, too. She missed him and needed his assurance that everything was going well. The disguise tonight had just been a game, to see if she could do it, but tomorrow would be the real thing. Tomorrow she would make contact with Dr. Orgutsov and things would start happening in a hurry. Her every move was being watched, so she had to be very careful. To implicate the doctor too early could start a series of events which would prevent them from leaving the country. Karen didn't know how much the KGB knew, but if she was seen with Orgutsov, they could begin to put things together fast. She shivered from the cold, but wanted to remain out in the air a few minutes longer. Tomorrow would require clear thinking.

Alex was closer than Karen could have imagined. While she was on the veranda, he walked through the lobby and took the elevator to his room on the fourth floor. Twice Alex had considered asking at the front desk for Karen, but did not want to attract any undue attention to her presence there. He knew there was a good chance she was in the hotel. That was what their schedule had called for, but she had no way of knowing he had come this far west to meet her. Alex had glanced into the dining area on his way upstairs, in the hopes Karen was there, but he didn't see her. He would just have to wait until morning to meet with her.

In his room, Alex rehashed the afternoon and his time spent with Dr. Orgutsov. It appeared Karen had read the man correctly. He was an extremely conscientious physician who was dedicated to saving his fellow man. Though not entirely at odds with his government, Orgutsov was disillusioned with the Communists and believed strongly his discovery would be better off in the hands of the Americans. Orgutsov had not said any of this to Alex, but it had been obvious from his manner with the American. Alex wondered how the doctor would feel once he learned what their plan was to get him to America.

That night Karen and Alex slept directly above and below one another in the hotel. Alex had traveled nearly 8,000 miles to get there. He had been traveling for seven days. Karen's journey had taken her over 12,000 miles, and she had started three days before Alex had begun his journey. Each of them had seen parts of the earth most Americans never dream of seeing. Yet sightseeing had not been on their minds. Alex's journey had been initiated by a highly secretive government agency using an ultra-modern method of subliminal communication. They had implanted within his mind the need and the will to go, as well as the plan. How they had done it was a mystery to him—a mystery he intended to solve as soon as he got home.

Karen's presence was due to her special knowledge in the field of internal medicine and a tremendous commitment to the well-being of her fellow man. Whoever had orchestrated the mission had played upon the special talents of the two people and their very unique friendship. Their ability to work together on this type of mission, unfettered by government regulations and red tape, and their combined resourcefulness made their being in the Soviet Union at this place and time meaningful. Neither would have had it any other way. It was right for Alex and it was right for Karen. They could only pray it was right for Orgutsov as well, and for the millions of lives that would be saved if they were successful.

Dmitri Flerov was in a quandary. Karen Webster had eluded him for at least two hours that evening. He had no idea what she was up to and finding out was very important to him. His superior in the KGB, Colonel Veektor Zhukov, wanted to know what the woman was doing in their country and it would serve Flerov's interests well to not only find out, but to stop it if it was something illegal. Upon learning of Karen Webster's connection with the former American agent, Alex Davis, Colonel Zhukov had become obsessed with learning of her mission. He had demanded to know her every move and had seemed disappointed to find her conduct appeared to be nothing more or less than that of an American tourist.

Two things had reinforced Zhukov's suspicion that her presence in Russia was more than it appeared. The first was Karen's aloofness where Flerov was concerned. It was a sharp contrast to her openness with Anna and what was reported to be her nature. It was known that Dr. Webster had always seemed to enjoy meeting men and getting to know them. Flerov had been courteous to her and had done everything he knew to attract her interest, yet she had rebuffed him. The other item was Karen's disappearance that afternoon. It could have been she had just stepped out to walk along the streets of the city, but it appeared more as if she had deliberately tried to avoid them. If that were so, then Karen Webster knew she was being watched and it had seemed important to her she prove she could elude any shadowing.

Though aggravated, Zhukov was not yet worried. There was no way she could leave the country undetected. What really bothered him was how in spite of all of their computer intelligence and his and Flerov's own mental gymnastics, neither of them had the slightest idea what she was up to. In Moscow, Zhukov had initiated numerous computer searches, using both the KGB computers and those of the GRU. He had his counterparts in Washington digging into Karen's activities since her previous trip to Russia a few weeks earlier. He was tracking her route within the Soviet Union for any scheduled political activities or dissident persons she might come into contact with. He would come up with the answer. He just hoped it would be soon enough to catch her at whatever anti-Soviet act she had come to commit.

Karen had trouble deciding on the morning she was to board the train to Jakutsk, just how she should dress. To board the train as Karen Webster would insure she would still have a tail. That would most likely jeopardize Dr. Orgutsov if she tried to meet with him. If she boarded in disguise, she might be successful in leaving her pursuers behind—for a time anyway. There were two negatives to that plan she could think of. One was when Karen Webster did not appear in Krasnojarsk, they would have real reason to be suspicious and would be that much more on the alert. The other was her registered travel plans had called for her to leave Krasnojarsk for Jakutsk on this day and to do otherwise would cause her to be in legitimate trouble with the authorities.

Then there was the problem of approaching Orgutsov. He would recognize Karen Webster, but in disguise she would not be familiar to him. With her limited knowledge of his language, that could present a real problem. As it was, even as Karen Webster, she would have to wait until Alex was present to explain their plan to Dr. Orgutsov.

Karen decided to board as herself, but just in case, she made some extra preparations. The day was cool and rainy, so she wore her beige London Fog raincoat. Underneath it was the simple skirt, white blouse and man's sweater she had worn to the restaurant the previous evening. Over her shoes she wore simple black rubber boots. She carried a big bag over her arm which contained the rest of the essentials that would be necessary for a quick change in identity, should it become necessary. Satisfied, she went to the lobby to request transportation to the train station.

Five minutes before Karen came down, Alex and Dr. Orgutsov had walked out of the restaurant, picked up their bags, and hailed a taxi for the train station. Alex had been continuously on the lookout for Karen, expecting her to appear any minute, yet not really wanting her to. In the hotel lobby there were too few people for a greeting between the American doctor and two Soviet citizens to go unnoticed. On the train, they could be much more isolated and could talk in the privacy of their first class compartment. Karen saw Dmitri Flerov in the hotel lobby, but he had hardly seemed to notice her. He was talking with a younger man she took to be KGB also. If they had followed her, she had not observed it.

In fact, they had not. Flerov had walked over to the telephone and placed a call to Moscow where Zhukov had been waiting. "She has gone to the train station, Comrade Colonel Zhukov," Flerov reported, "It is our driver who has taken her."

"Was she alone?" Zhukov asked. "What of the Ministry of Health official, Dr. Orgutsov. Was he with her?" Zhukov's computer searches had finally turned up one possible link, although a weak one. This Doctor Lev Orgutsov had been a lecturer at the medical convention which Karen Webster had attended on her previous trip into the Soviet Union. He was now on a state-sponsored speaking tour that coincided with the American doctor's travels. Was it a coincidence, or was there something more here? Zhukov was not sure, but it was the only thing he had come up with and it was worth exploring. While Orgutsov was not known as a dissident, it was felt within party circles he was on to something much more important than he led his superiors to believe.

Orgutsov had been involved in cancer research for years and had apparently cured many patients. When asked how he had done it, he had continually denied any major breakthrough and had declared that the healings, while extremely fortunate, had been just freak accidents. The real cure for cancer, he had repeatedly told the Ministry of Health officials, was still years away. Yet at the same time, his requests for funding for new materials and research had slowed and his reports had begun to appear repetitive. It was as if he was stalling for some reason. Zhukov was hypothesizing Karen Webster was part of that reason. If he could pinpoint the two of them together, he might have something to go on, but there had to be something else, too, something he could not see yet.

"No, Comrade Colonel Zhukov, but Orgutsov was here a few minutes earlier, along with a colleague, and the two of them left for the train before Karen Webster came down from her room."

"A colleague? What colleague? There is no record he is traveling with any colleague."

"I checked the registry, Comrade Colonel. He is Dr. Yuri Yaralov, also of the Ministry of Health."

"Very interesting. Get to the train station and get on that train. Stay with them, but do not be obvious. I am flying to Jakutsk and will meet you there."

"Very well, Comrade Colonel Zhukov." Flerov hung up the telephone and he and his companion stepped out to the curb where a KGB car was waiting to take them to the station. Zhukov had already called for a computer search on Yaralov. It took him less than fifteen minutes to determine no such person existed within the Ministry of Health. Perhaps Flerov had been mistaken about his affiliation, but then again, perhaps this was the key he was looking for. Zhukov's instincts told him finding the identity of this third traveler, whoever he was, was vital toward thwarting whatever plan was being carried out. He put all of the resources available to him onto the task of finding out who this Yaralov was. Then he started his preparations for travel. Jakutsk was a long way from Moscow.

15

Karen boarded the train and walked through the first class coach to her compartment. Suddenly she gasped! There, in one of the compartments on the left side of the train, facing the direction from which she had come, sat Alex and Dr. Orgutsov. Alex very imperceptibly shook his head from side to side. Once, but it was enough. Karen then realized she had stopped in the aisle of the train and stood there with her mouth hanging open. It had been very unprofessional of her, and the type of thing Alex had warned her about that could get her in trouble. Quickly, she moved on and found her compartment.

Fortunately, she was alone in the compartment. She quickly located a porter and had him assist her in converting the compartment into a sleeping berth. Then she drew the curtains around her. She was trembling. Alex was there and she had almost blown it! She didn't know how far behind her Flerov or his associate might be, but he could have been watching, or he could even have someone else on her tail now, someone she had not identified.

At any rate, she had to be extremely careful, for now they would surely be watched if she was seen with Alex and Dr. Orgutsov. Yet how could she stay away. Alex was here! They had traveled so far to get to this point. She never had dreamed he would come this far west. How had he managed it? Where was the plane? And Alex was with Orgutsov. That was supposed to be her job. How had he managed that? Did Alex even need her now, or would her presence here be a hindrance to him? There was so much she wanted to ask him. She just wanted to be with him. She wanted her heart to stop pounding, and she wanted to know what to do next. She couldn't just sit here on this train and do nothing.

Suddenly, she had an idea. Alex might not like it, but by the time he found out about it, it would be too late. Besides, she couldn't ask him, could she? In the privacy of her berth, Karen transformed herself into the darkhaired, plainly dressed Russian woman who had dined in the Yenisey Hotel dining room the previous evening. She emerged from the berth and satisfied that neither Flerov nor his young associate were around, reclosed the curtains and made her way back to where Alex and Dr. Orgutsov were seated. She entered their compartment and sat down opposite them. She waited for Alex to speak first. She needed him to set the tone of their meeting. It was all she could do to keep from throwing her arms around him, she was so glad to see him.

Alex spoke in Russian. "Dr. Orgutsov, say hello to Dr. Webster." Orgutsov looked surprised.

"But this is not Karen Webster," Orgutsov began. Then seeing her smile and turning to notice the amusement in Alex's eyes, he realized she was in disguise. "Of course, my dear. How clever of you. We should now be able to talk very freely. Your friend, Dr. Yaralov, tells me you have something of interest to talk with me about."

Quickly, Karen introduced Alex. Then she explained their purpose and their plan while Alex translated. As she talked, Orgutsov continued to shake his head and smile in amazement. From time to time he would lower his forehead into the palm of his hand, his elbow resting on his knee and shake his head from side to side. "Lady, lady," was his only comment as Alex translated what Karen was saying. Neither of them were sure they knew how to read his reaction to their scheme. For all they knew, he could blow the whistle on them any minute. Finally, they stopped talking and waited for his reaction. The grayhaired Russian doctor sat back in his seat and rubbed his chin. Finally, he cleared his throat and began to speak. Karen couldn't understand many of the words, but she thought she detected a slight twinkle in his eyes. As Alex translated, she knew she had been right.

"I knew when I first saw you and read of your works, young lady, you were a resourceful person. Somehow I knew I could trust my dream to you—my dream of coming to America with what I have learned so everyone might benefit from it. I even had some hope you could help me. I don't know, perhaps I was somehow directed, as if some mastermind were behind this entire scheme and my meeting you in Moscow at the convention was no accident. But this is incredible. I never dreamed you could come up with a plan that could make my dream a reality in such a short time."

"Why," Karen asked, "if you did not believe I could, or would, do anything with it, did you give me your itinerary and the notes from your discoveries?"

"I don't know, Dr. Webster, perhaps it was what you call intuition, or perhaps, like I said, this whole thing has been devised by some mastermind that somehow planted the thoughts in my head. I don't know why I did it, but I am certainly glad I did."

"Then you will come with us?" Karen asked.

"My dear, I wouldn't miss it for the world. But there is just one thing."

"What is it?" Alex asked. Karen was trying unsuccessfully to follow what was being said.

"I am terrified of flying. Why else would I be riding this train all over the country?"

Karen smiled as Alex translated for her. Surely, they could overcome that small problem. With all of the other obstacles they conceivably had before them, this one seemed small.

Alex was thinking about what Orgutsov had said about someone masterminding the whole thing. Had CAFI's influence been working on this end, too? Had the agency so perfected the subliminal techniques they had used on Alex they were able to use them here, too? If so, the possibilities were endless. If they could communicate subliminally to Russian officials in their native language, they could change the entire direction of the Russian government. The potential was mindboggling. "They've come a long way, baby," was all Alex could think of.

16

Flerov and his young associate, Armen Sarvazyan, boarded the train just before it pulled out from the station. They did not take the time to locate Karen, knowing they had almost 24 hours of travel ahead of them before the train reached Jakutsk. Instead, they went to their compartment and set up a chessboard. Perhaps if they had noticed the woman in the compartment with Orgutsov and the man they knew as Yaralov, they would have been suspicious. On the other hand, they might have taken her as just another passenger. At any rate, neither one of them was concerned about it now. They knew neither Karen Webster nor Dr. Orgutsov was expected to leave the train before reaching Jakutsk, many miles ahead. They would locate Dr. Webster before the first intermediate stop to make sure she did not alter her plans.

In their compartment, Karen, Alex and Dr. Orgutsov were going over their plans to escape the Soviet Union. Orgutsov had no immediate family, so there was no one he regretted leaving behind. He had been married once, but the marriage had ended in divorce years earlier and he had lost track of his former wife. He would be missed if he did not make his scheduled visit to Jakutsk, and he would be missed at the Ministry of Health Academy in Moscow. How long it would take the KGB to realize he was in America, he did not know.

Karen wanted to know the details of Alex's trip and what faced them on their trip back to the States. They were still so deep within Russia, the magnitude of the task before them was intimidating to Karen. Alex was confident they could get to the plane undetected and he kept telling Karen to relax. Dr. Orgutsov was not worried about getting to Magadan, but he was already nervous about the plane ride. He decided to retire to his berth and leave Karen and Alex together for a while.

As soon as Orgutsov was gone, Karen moved across the open space between them and sat next to Alex. She put her head on his shoulder. "Oh, Alex, I'm really scared," she said.

Alex put his arm around her and held her close. "We've got a lot of miles ahead of us, little lady, so you've got to keep your cool. Now tell me about this Dmitri Flerov and whoever else you think might be tailing you." Karen sat up and told Alex about Anna, and about seeing her with Flerov. She told him about his slip-up in calling her Dr. Webster and about how she had first put on her disguise back at the hotel in Krasnojarsk and had fooled him. She had not seen Flerov on the train yet, but was sure he was probably on it. She told him about Flerov's younger companion. Alex wanted to know if she would recognize him. Karen was sure she would.

For several minutes, Alex thought about the significance of Flerov and the other agents. The fact at least three people had been involved in Karen's surveillance indicated someone with political clout was interested in her. That would make things more difficult as they traveled from Jakutsk to Magadan. Since there was no train that made the trip, they would have to travel by commercial air or by automobile. Obtaining an automobile might prove difficult. The only way they could travel by air would be if Karen maintained her disguise. As an American, he doubted she could buy a ticket which deviated from her planned itinerary without going through the government to get approval. That could take some time and would certainly call attention to her.

They had time to decide and Alex needed some of that time to think through possible alternatives. One alternative was for Karen to return to the United States commercially. Alex had felt that was the best plan at the beginning. Even now, since he had made contact with Orgutsov, Karen could return to Moscow by train or plane and fly to the United States. That would be the safest course for her except for one thing. If Alex and Orgutsov's departure were detected before she got out of the country, the Russians could and probably would, detain her. If she were with them, Alex could take care of her. He really hesitated to let her go on her own now. He would make up his mind before they reached Jakutsk.

Flerov and Sarvazyan finished their chess game and decided to stroll through the train to locate Orgutsov and Karen Webster. They separated, Flerov moving toward the front of the train and the younger agent checking the rear cars. It was Sarvazyan who went in the direction of the Americans. As he passed their compartment, he observed the man traveling with Dr. Orgutsov, the man identified as Dr. Yaralov. There was a woman with the doctor Sarvazyan had not seen before. She may have just been a traveler who happened to share the compartment, but the KGB agent thought it odd she was sitting beside the doctor rather than across from him. There was no sign of Dr. Orgutsov or Dr. Webster, but a number of the sleeping berths were occupied and it was possible they were resting. He returned to his compartment and reported his findings to Flerov.

Through the day, that night and into the next day, the two Americans traveled what seemed like an endless journey toward Magadan, alternately, and sometimes together, keeping company with Dr. Orgutsov, the Russian doctor they had come to take out of the Soviet Union. Karen removed her disguise and sat alone in her compartment long enough for Flerov to satisfy himself she had not gotten off at one of the interim stops the train made. At one small village, Flerov was able to make contact with Zhukov via phone. The latter had been on a layover on his way to Jakutsk. Zhukov had been particularly interested in the description of the man traveling with Dr.

Orgutsov and the woman who appeared to be with them. The phony ID of the other doctor was a mystery Zhukov must solve. Flerov wanted to confront the guy on the train and ask for his papers, but Zhukov disagreed. The papers would probably be in order because the man would be a professional. The train was no place to deal with the matter. Besides, he could be a real doctor and they could be mistaken about his being connected with the Academy of Medical Sciences. Zhukov intended to be in Jakutsk by the time the train arrived where he would see the man for himself.

As it turned out, Zhukov's flight was delayed due to mechanical problems and the train arrived in Jakutsk ahead of him. Karen went straight to the hotel and checked in with the Intourist desk in the lobby. She then went to her room, changed her appearance and her dress and went back outside to wait on the curb for Alex and Dr. Orgutsov. This time she had a different disguise, another one Alex had prepared for her. Instead of darkening her hair, she sprayed it silver. She wore a hat and a dark, knee-length coat. She wore no glasses and no makeup. She had a complete set of identity papers identifying her as a government mining official. When she appeared in the lobby and on the street, neither Flerov nor his associate was around.

Alex and Orgutsov picked Karen up in a hired car and headed to the airport. Alex had already called and made arrangements for the three of them to catch an afternoon flight to Magadan. The weather was miserable. It was a cold rainy afternoon and Orgutsov was already dreading the flight. He told the two Americans he sometimes managed to fly on an airliner, after stiffening himself with a few shots of vodka, but he did not know how he would react to the upcoming flight in the small airplane they were going to use to escape the country. Alex had finally decided to take Karen with them. There was too much risk involved in having her go all the way back through Moscow once it was determined he and Orgutsov were missing.

Leaving the car outside the terminal, the three made their way through ticketing to the waiting area. They waited with the other passengers under a shelter by the ramp. They watched as the plane they were to fly out on, arrived from the west and its passengers disembarked. The three huddled together, fighting off the chill as the de-planing passengers hurried to get out of the rain. Unknown to them, Colonel Veektor Zhukov, KGB, was one of those passengers. Waiting for him in a car outside the terminal were Dmitri Flerov and Armen Sarvazyan. As Zhukov ducked under the shelter, he found himself face to face with a ghost out of his past—Alex Davis! Alex gave no hint of recognition as he took the arms of his two companions and ushered them through the rain to the waiting plane.

Zhukov stood transfixed as he mentally tried to put the pieces together. Momentarily, he was torn. Alex Davis was dead! He had to have been mistaken. The man was traveling with another man and a woman, but the woman was not Karen Webster. As to Orgutsov, Zhukov had never seen the man, so he would not recognize him.

Quickly, he ran through the terminal, stopping long enough to check the destination of the plane now being loaded. He found Flerov outside the terminal and as he got into the back seat of the car he asked where Karen Webster, Lev Orgutsov and the third man were. Flerov assured his commander Dr. Webster had checked into her hotel and had gone to her room. Orgutsov and the other soviet doctor had hired a car and had headed in the direction of the hospital. The two KGB agents had barely had time to confirm the destination of the three people they were tailing before going to the airport to pick Colonel Zhukov up. They could now easily divide up and keep the three individuals under surveillance. Flerov was frankly beginning to think his commander had him on a wild goose chase. The American woman seemed harmless and the two Soviet doctors appeared to be on routine business.

Yet Zhukov was bothered by it all. First off, there was the mistaken identity, if that's what it was, of Orgutsov's traveling companion, Dr. Yuri Yaralov. Who was that man? Then there was the fact Karen Webster's schedule so closely matched that of Dr. Orgutsov, whom she had met little more than a month previously and who, it was suspected, held medical secrets that would be valuable to the Soviet Union in its bid to be the dominant world power. But what really bothered him was the man at the airport. If he had not been so sure Alex Davis was dead and his look-alike, Major Grigory Kotosvk, was now in hiding in America, he would have been sure Davis was behind all of this. Quickly, he had the two agents drive him to the hospital. He wanted to get a firsthand look at this mystery man, Yuri Yuralov.

They arrived at the hospital and went inside, inquiring at the administrator's office for Dr. Lev Orgutsov. They were told he was scheduled to be there that morning but had not yet arrived. "You fools!" Zhukov snarled. "Take me to Karen Webster, now!"

The KGB agents raced the Volga across town to the hotel. All three went inside, and after checking the registry, proceeded to Karen's room. They knocked and received no answer, so they summoned the hotel manager to let them in the room. There was no sign of Karen or any of her luggage. Quickly, Zhukov phoned the airport. The plane for Magadan had left 45 minutes earlier and there was not another plane scheduled until the next day at the same time.

Zhukov was furious. His KGB agents had grown complacent and let their charges give them the slip. There had to be only one answer. The man he had seen at the airport *was* Alex Davis *or* Grigory Kotosvk and the two with him had been Karen Webster and the Soviet physician, Lev Orgutsov. But why were they going to Magadan? And how could he beat them there?

They drove to the GRU headquarters in the center of the city. The KGB did not have an office in this town, since it was so far inland. Colonel Zhukov used the GRU computer to pull up a profile on Alex Davis and Grigory Kotosvk. The computer showed Kotosvk had been killed ten years earlier, but Zhukov believed it had been Davis. He showed the computer-generated photograph to Flerov and Sarvazyan who looked at it carefully. This could have been the man who was with Orgutsov. Of course the man in the picture was much younger, he was leaner and his hair was darker and cut much shorter. After careful study, the two conceded it probably was the man they had seen on the train. The woman Zhukov had seen did not match the description of either Karen Webster or the woman on the train with Orgutsov and the man Zhukov now believed was Alex Davis.

Zhukov went into a private office and shut the door. He had to think. Could he possibly have been wrong ten years ago? He had been so sure then he had gotten Davis, that perhaps his follow-up investigation had not been as thorough as warranted. Yet Davis had not shown up anywhere since. With Davis out of the way, there had been plenty for him to concentrate on. Now he had to go to Magadan and find them. In fact, if he could get a military jet, he might be able to beat the Aeroflot turboprop to the eastern city. Zhukov picked up the phone and got a patch into Air Force Headquarters.

17

After boarding the Soviet airliner, Alex, Karen and Orgutsov split up. Karen took a seat on the right-hand side of the plane, near the front. Dr. Orgutsov seated himself in an aisle seat halfway down on the left. Alex moved to the rear of the plane and waited before sitting down to see if Zhukov boarded. The momentary confrontation on the ramp had caused Alex some alarm. Instantly his trained reflexes had taken over and he had avoided giving himself away. Nevertheless, the chance of recognition was high. In years gone by, Zhukov had hounded Alex with a passion. He alone had come close to exposing Alex's real identity on several occasions. The fact Alex had outwitted him every time had only served to fuel Zhukov's anger and make the KGB agent that much more of an adversary. Was it coincidence he had been on the ramp? Alex didn't think so. If Zhukov was in Jakutsk at the same time he and Karen were there, he had to be on to something.

Alex fully expected Zhukov to board the plane and attempt to arrest him. He had hurriedly briefed Karen and Orgutsov as the three of them had run through the rain to board the waiting Ilyushin airliner. He would act as a decoy. If Zhukov came aboard the plane and attempted to confront Alex, Dr. Orgutsov was to stay aboard and feign innocence. There was nothing to connect him with the two Americans. Karen was to exit, via the front stairs, take a cab back to the hotel and reappear as Karen Webster, continuing her vacation. Alex would either attempt to escape, or confront the KGB Colonel head on, depending upon the circumstances. As it turned out, the plan was unnecessary, for the cabin doors closed and the aircraft began to taxi without any sign of Zhukov.

Alex knew this wasn't over. He surmised the Soviet agent had hesitated out of uncertainty and in hesitating, had missed his chance. He would be quick to put together the pieces, however, and now their race out of the country would be just that—a race. As the airliner took off on its journey eastward, Alex, Karen and Lev Orgutsov exchanged glances of relief. Only after they leveled off did Alex allow himself to relax, but then only briefly. Within a few minutes, his mind was once again engaged, planning the steps they would take once they reached Magadan. Getting to the Eagle and getting airborne were only part of the tasks which lay ahead of them. He must get them safely over many miles of Soviet soil, plus avoid being discovered entering his own country. They could just as easily be shot down by an F-15 as they could a Russian MIG, especially with the Eagle wearing the Soviet star.

18

Susan Davis answered the phone in her bedroom after the first ring. On edge for days, she had been anxiously awaiting some word from Alex, something just to let her know he was all right, he was on his way home, and she would be seeing him again soon.

"Mrs. Davis, my name is J. L. McDaniels. Do you know where Alex is?" The voice on the other end of the phone was unfamiliar to Susan; the name was not.

"No I don't know, Mr. McDaniels, but tell me you are somehow involved in whatever he is doing."

"Perhaps we had better talk, Susan. Obviously, you know who I am," McDaniels said.

"Yes, sir, I know who you are, but it wasn't Alex who told me. I want you to know that," Susan replied.

"It doesn't really matter now, Susan. I'll make some flight arrangements and call you right back. If you can meet me at the airport, perhaps we can talk there."

"Sure," Susan responded, "that'll be fine. I'll wait to hear from you." As she put down the telephone receiver, Susan felt tears welling up in her eyes. Then she began to sob, her body shaking uncontrollably. She was glad the kids weren't around to see her, but just as she thought about it, Mary came into the room to see what was the matter.

"What's wrong, Mommy," she asked. "Is it Daddy? He's all right, isn't he?"

Mary ran into her mother's arms and Susan held her close. Stroking the little girl's head, she replied, "I don't know, Mary. I guess he's all right, but I don't know for sure. Oh, I wish I knew where Karen was. She could tell me. She helped Alex plan whatever he's doing, I know she did."

Susan arrested her tears for her daughter's sake. Getting up, she went into the bathroom and washed her face. "I'm sorry, Mary. He's all right, I know he is. It's just he's been gone so long and there's been no word. It's not like your daddy not to tell me what he's doing. He just told me I would have to trust him, that's all. The men who work with him don't know where he is. Karen probably knows, but I don't know where she is or how to get in touch with her. There is a man flying in to meet me who seems to have some news about your father, but I don't know if it's good news or bad. I'm trying to be strong, Mary, like I know your father wants me to, but it's so hard."

"I know, Mommy. Don't cry. Daddy can take care of himself. You know he can."

"Yes, Mary, he can. Now run along and play. I have to get ready to go to the airport to meet this friend of your father's."

"Yes, ma'am," Mary replied.

As Mary left, Susan began putting on her makeup. She had not been out of the house much since Alex had been gone and was mad at herself for letting her appearance slip. She was usually careful to present a good image, one Alex would be proud of. Within a few minutes, McDaniels called her back. He would be in at 7:00 o'clock that evening, which was still a few hours away. Susan was embarrassed she didn't know any more about Alex's activities than she did. She decided to get as much information as she could before her meeting with Alex's former boss. If McDaniels had approached her openly about Alex, it must be important.

Susan decided to call Karen's housekeeper, Consuelo, to see if she knew where Karen could be reached. The housekeeper was just as frustrated with her boss as Susan was with her husband. Then calling Karen's office, she got the same response. No one knew exactly where she was vacationing and she had not written or called.

Neither Bud Ewing nor Ken Webb had any idea where Alex was. Bud was anxious to get the Eagle back and would have a few choice words to say to his business partner when he returned. For a fleeting moment, Susan began to weigh the surmounting evidence that Karen and Alex had run away together. Quickly, she shook that thought from her mind. It was out of character for both of them. They were both painfully honest people. No, if that were to happen, at least they would have had the decency to tell her. Besides, as long as she had known them, there had been no romantic involvement between them. They were too much like brother and sister. Still, there was the nagging question Susan sometimes had about why Karen had never married.

Later, at the airport as she met J. L. McDaniels, Susan knew nothing more than she had earlier when she had talked to him on the phone. McDaniels was obviously familiar with Susan's appearance, for he walked right up to her in the waiting crowd and introduced himself. A rather common looking man in his late fifties, with gray hair and a paunch, he didn't at all look like the head of a secret government spy agency. He was nothing like Susan had pictured him. She wondered if she should tell him how she had come to know who he was, but decided against it.

It had been Karen who had told her the story, during one of those intimate conversations women tend to have when they are pouring the contents of their hearts out to one another. Karen had made Susan promise not to tell Alex she knew, but there was a trust the two women had developed as Susan had come to understand Karen's relationship to her husband. Sharing what she knew with Susan was the only way Karen knew to keep that trust.

McDaniels and Susan went into one of the airport coffee shops and sat in an isolated corner where they could talk. They ordered something to eat and J. L. waited until the waitress was through serving before getting down to the details of why he had come to see Susan.

"Susan, you must forgive me for intruding into your private life like this. It is something Alex would detest and he has told me so on more than one occasion. The fact you know who I am makes my inquiries somewhat easier. I know Alex did not tell you about me or about CAFI, so I can only surmise you and Karen Webster share some secrets. The fact is I am very concerned for Alex and Karen's safety for reasons I will tell you in a moment. First, you must tell me everything you can about their departure and their activities immediately prior to their going. Also, you must try to remember anything and everything you can Alex told you before he left that might give me a clue to go on."

"Perhaps," Susan replied, "you could tell *me* what you know first. That might jog my memory by giving me something to relate to."

"Very well," McDaniels replied, pausing to take a bite out of his club sandwich. Susan hardly touched her food. She was too concerned with learning something of her husband's whereabouts to think about food now. McDaniels ate as if this meal might be the last he would have for a while. Judging from his appearance, he probably ate most of his meals that way. Susan wished he would stop worrying about his food and get down to details. "Within the last few days, the KGB network within this country has been very actively seeking information about Karen. Just this morning, there began to be inquiries about Alex as well. That information by itself would not have triggered much of an alarm except our own agents within the Soviet Union have stumbled upon something, quite by accident I might add, that seems to tie it all together. Alex and Karen Webster are in Russia this very moment and are stirring up some fairly high level curiosity.

"Within the last few hours there has been an increased level of activity that indicates the KGB is seeking Alex or the man Alex impersonated on several occasions while in the Soviet Union, a Major Grigory Kotosvk. Kotosvk is dead, but evidently someone thinks it was Alex who died instead. I haven't put all of the pieces together yet, Susan, but it's beginning to look like Alex and Karen may need my help and I need to know how I can help them. I am hoping you can help me fill in some of the details."

Susan was stunned. Alex in Russia! That thought had not occurred to her. But there was no reason it would have. Karen had made the trip almost two months earlier, and when she had gotten back, there had been something she had been anxious to share with Alex. Yet neither of them had ever mentioned to her what it was. She knew the two of them had spent a lot of time together in the last few weeks, but Alex had not indicated anything to her which would have made her think they were planning a trip together. Why would they go to Russia? What could they possibly hope to accomplish, and how had Alex gotten there?

"Mr. McDaniels," Susan began, "Alex and Karen spent a lot of time together after she returned from a medical convention in Moscow. He made a couple of trips out of town which were unexpected and for which he never told me the reason. The last one was to New Orleans. When he left, he told me he was going to Alaska and he went in a new plane his company had recently purchased. Actually, it isn't a new plane, but an old one. It's a rather unique airplane called the Windecker Eagle. Alex and his business partner have been using it to test some sort of device they are hoping to sell to the military. No one connected with either Alex or Karen seems to know where they went, and no one has heard from either of them in almost two weeks.

"Before Karen went to Russia, Alex had been acting a little distant. He seemed preoccupied much of the time. All of that changed when Karen returned. It was as if he had a purpose and that purpose was wrapped up in something only Alex and Karen knew about. I tried to find out, but I learned nothing. Alex told me what he was doing was important and I would just have to trust him. He said it would all be over very soon. The last time I talked with him was the night after he left. He called me from Canada. Until today, I thought Karen was vacationing in Europe. Alex and I even drove her to the airport."

Susan unloaded all of her information at once and McDaniels listened intently. There were a few clues in what she had told him, clues he hoped would help him unlock the rest of the puzzle. He hoped he could fill in the missing pieces quickly, for his instincts told him Alex was in trouble and right now McDaniels didn't have the slightest idea how he or CAFI could help him.

The connection with Karen Webster's trip to Moscow, the Windecker Eagle and the trip to New Orleans all offered hope. Perhaps Phuoc could fill in some missing pieces. If Alex was in Russia and had made a trip to New Orleans, Phuoc and his shop had to have been in his travel plans. J. L. thanked Susan and promised to let her know immediately if he uncovered any more information. He gave her his private telephone number and told her to call him immediately if she heard from Alex or remembered anything else that might help. Then he boarded a flight back to San Antonio.

19

The military plane Zhukov summoned would not arrive in Jakutsk early enough to allow him to beat the Aeroflot flight to Magadan. The best he could hope for was to arrive in the eastern Siberian city within 30 minutes of Alex Davis' arrival. He made arrangements by telephone to have KGB agents in Magadan to meet the plane and follow the trio.

Zhukov, Flerov and Sarvazyan were waiting at the Jakutsk Airport when the plane arrived that would take them to Magadan. As they settled aboard the aircraft, Zhukov briefed his companions. "Unfortunately, we still do not know what the Americans are up to. Perhaps we will know by the time we reach Magadan. The presence of Kotosvk or Davis, whichever one it is, complicates matters greatly. Either of them could steal one of our military aircraft from the airfield at Magadan. They must know for sure I will be after them, so they will be very alert. Davis is a master at eluding discovery. The other two are rank amateurs and should be very easy to pick up. Let us hope we can reach them before they make any trouble, eh?" The other two just nodded in agreement. Neither of them was very inclined to raise any questions with their superior at this moment.

Alex knew the situation was critical. It was almost impossible for him to communicate with Karen and Orgutsov to the extent necessary while the plane was airborne, yet he had to have a plan once they reached Magadan. There would be someone at the airport watching for them. It was possible they could give whoever it was the slip by remaining separated. Neither Karen nor Dr. Orgutsov had been seen closely by Zhukov so their descriptions might not have been accurately relayed. That Zhukov himself could beat them to Magadan was something Alex recognized as possible, yet he doubted it. At best they would have only a few minutes to get safely through the terminal and lost in the city. Reaching into his pocket, Alex pulled out a small notebook from which he tore two sheets of paper. On each of the pieces of paper he wrote an address in Russian. It was the only address in Magadan he could remember: that of the Intourist Hotel, which was near the downtown district. When he had finished writing, Alex folded the two pieces of paper and getting up from his seat, walked down the aisle and discreetly handed one to Dr. Orgutsov and one to Karen. Then he returned to his seat and waited for the flight to end.

The two GRU agents assigned the airport detail were unsure of their mission. Supposedly they were to locate and tail three people traveling together. It was some KGB matter they had been called in on. The trio they were to locate consisted of two men and a woman, yet they had only been given a description of the two men. The GRU agents were not to detain the three travelers, but to follow them to their destination within the city and report that destination back to headquarters while they stood guard. They would be joined by KGB agents shortly.

The two agents' confusion was compounded when the plane landed and the policemen detected no one traveling together who fit the descriptions they had been given. By the time they had located and identified one of the men, the other two travelers had apparently slipped into the terminal and obtained their luggage. Upon realizing the three travelers had split up, the two Soviet agents quickly decided one of them should follow the man they had recognized while the other one tried to find at least one of the other two travelers. There were three women traveling alone on the plane, plus several more who appeared to be with their husbands or families. Which was the woman they were after? Undecided, they located Dr. Orgutsov and one followed him while the other attempted to follow Alex. Alex went into the men's room with his luggage, but did not come back out. After waiting outside for a few minutes and seeing no one but an Air Force pilot come through the door, the agent went inside the restroom only to find it empty. His charge had given him the slip!

Dr. Orgutsov hailed a taxi. The agent following him crossed the street to his car and fell in behind the taxi as it traveled across town. The other agent stepped outside the air terminal just in time to see the Air Force pilot get into a taxi. He could have been the same man! The appearance was similar. Unsure of the identification, the Soviet looked around again to try to locate the woman. Should he follow the pilot? Weighing his alternatives, he decided something was better than nothing. He ran to his car to follow the Air Force officer.

Karen watched Dr. Orgutsov and Alex leave and saw the two men following them. She had apparently remained undetected. In order to make sure, she walked to the far end of the terminal before approaching a waiting taxi. Getting in, she looked around to verify she was not being followed. Then she handed the slip of paper with the address on it to the driver. During the ride into the business district, Karen continued to watch behind her. She was concerned about Alex and about Dr. Orgutsov. Suppose the three all arrived at the hotel at the same time and were discovered. The fact she was not being followed seemed academic to her. As soon as she rejoined the other two, their chances of being picked up would be greatly increased. Alex probably had a plan, he always seemed to. As for her part, Karen decided the best thing she could do would be to check into the hotel under her mining official identity and wait for Alex to contact her.

Alex had seen Dr. Orgutsov's pursuer as well as his own. He didn't know about Karen. When he last saw her standing alone at the airport terminal, she did not appear to have a tail. His decoying tactics had worked at least partially. The next step would depend upon how professional the two men following Dr. Orgutsov and him were and how far they had been given permission to act. When he arrived at the hotel, he saw Dr. Orgutsov checking in. Alex decided to wait in the lobby for Karen and follow her to her room. He did not see any point in getting a room himself. They wouldn't be there that long. As soon as they could shake themselves free of their pursuers, they would hire or steal a car and get to the Eagle. It was time to get out of this country!

The two agents Alex had spotted at the airport terminal entered the hotel lobby in a hurry, their eyes searching the room until they located the men they were looking for. Alex was standing where he could easily be spotted. Orgutsov was just stepping onto the elevator and one of the agents headed that way quickly, trying to catch the door. The other crossed the lobby to the registration table, apparently to confirm the man's identity and locate his room number. That gave Alex the chance to stroll outside where he hoped to intercept Karen before she came inside. He waited for a moment or two near the front door, then began walking in the direction from which the cab would most likely approach. His mind was on locating transportation and he hoped at least one of the Soviet agents had been careless enough to leave his car unlocked. Both of the black Volgas were parked at the curb. The first one he approached was unlocked. In fact, the key was in the ignition.

Alex hesitated only a moment before reaching to open the door. Looking around quickly, he saw two things that stopped him. One was the Soviet agent who appeared on the sidewalk outside the hotel door. He was the man who had checked the hotel registration and now he was obviously trying to relocate Alex. The other was Karen, who was getting out of a taxi in front of the hotel. Alex turned to approach the man, distracting him so he would take no notice of Karen. Behind the man, Karen briefly looked at Alex, then went inside. Alex walked up to the Soviet agent, catching him off guard. "Comrade," Alex said, "You must be more careful with the property of the state. You left your keys in the ignition."

"Yes, Comrade Major, I will," said the man, obviously confused at the bold approach of this man who was supposed to be his adversary. "I was just coming out to get them."

"I wonder," Alex said, "If you might be going near the Central District sometime soon. I am to meet there with members of the military registry and I could use a ride."

The man hesitated, as if to say no. Then it came to him if this was one of the men he was to follow, how better to discover his destination within the city than to take him there. "I am at your service, Comrade Major. Please get in." Alex opened the passenger door of the small car and got in as the other man walked around to the driver's side. This might be the opportunity he needed. Alex did not want to hurt the man unnecessarily, but he needed transportation and this black Volga would not attract any undue attention if he could successfully obtain it without calling attention to himself.

As they rode through the city streets, Alex watched for an opportunity, but decided it wasn't going to be easy. There were people all around and there seemed to be no legitimate excuse to get off the beaten path. He was running out of time and the ideas running through his mind were being discarded one by one. He thought of faking sickness and having the man pull over. When the agent was distracted, Alex could knock him unconscious and steal the car. But how would he dispose of him in a way that would not attract attention and would buy him the time he needed to get back to the hotel, pick up his companions and get out of the city? He could lure the man into a building, overpower him and steal the keys, but then he still had the problem of putting the Soviet out of commission for a considerable length of time. Finally, as they approached the government district, Alex decided on the direct approach. He would gain the man as an ally.

"Comrade, do you know who I am and why you were sent to follow me?" Alex asked.

"No," said the young man, shaking his head and obviously wary of a trap.

"I am Vladimir Glotser, GRU Colonel." Alex reached into his jacket pocket and brought out a set of identification papers which he thrust at the young agent driving the car. The man looked at them quickly, but could not take his eyes off the road because of the traffic. Alex was playing the odds this man was GRU rather than KGB and was counting on the rivalry between the two state-run security agencies. In theory, the two police agencies should complement one another—the one concerned with internal security, while the other was charged with policing the borders and Soviet activities abroad.

Alex had surmised the KGB presence would be minuscule in this far eastern city and Zhukov would have to depend upon GRU help, whether he wanted to or not. "Do you know who Colonel Veektor Zhukov, KGB, is?" Alex continued. Again the man shook his head.

"I do not know whether to take you into my confidence or not," Alex told the man, "but there is so much at stake I feel I must take a chance and solicit your help." The young agent's curiosity was obviously being raised as Alex spoke. "I have been working for months to uncover an organization of dissidents who have been selling high level military secrets to the West. The two people I was traveling with are part of that organization. They trust me and believe I am one of them. We came here for a meeting in which I planned to uncover their activities and have them arrested with evidence in their possession that will convict them. Zhukov is an opportunist who puts his own career above the welfare of the state." This last phrase Alex spoke with obvious contempt for the man. He hoped to turn the young Soviet agent against him too.

"Zhukov is planning on butting in and taking all of the credit for himself. The problem is, he will act prematurely and probably come on the scene before the evidence is in the open. He hopes to make the KGB look good at the expense of the GRU. However, nothing will be accomplished by his actions and my months of work will have been in vain."

"Yes, Comrade Colonel," answered the Soviet agent. "The KGB does tend to interfere where it is not needed." Alex was relieved. He had guessed right.

"So, tell me, Comrade, are you GRU as well?" Alex asked. When the man nodded, Alex responded, "Good. Perhaps you can help me."

"What can I do?" the man asked.

"Start driving back toward the hotel," Alex answered. "I will explain to you what we must do." Alex knew he had to include the man in his plan in a way that would make him feel he could obtain personal recognition for helping to expose such important anti-Soviet activity. Carefully, he laid out the plot in a way that had the young GRU agent playing a vital role. Alex managed to convince him of the importance of keeping Zhukov in the background until the right time.

As they drove up in front of the hotel, Alex told the agent to brief his companion while he went up to get the other two members of his party. "Tell him to wait here until he hears from you. The two of you can bring the KGB agents to the place I will show you when the time comes." The man agreed, then went over to talk to his companion. Alex stopped long enough to ask the room numbers of Dr. Orgutsov and the woman. The agent seemed surprised the woman was in the hotel. "Never mind," Alex said. "I will find her." He went to pick up a house phone and asked for the name Karen was traveling under. She picked up the phone on the first ring. "What's your room number?" Alex asked. After she gave it to him he told her to call Orgutsov and tell him to come to her room.

Alex went upstairs and knocked on Karen's door. She opened it immediately. She had changed clothes and was wearing a pair of slacks and a pullover sweater. Her hair was still silver. It was no longer pulled back, but was falling free, over her ears and touching the sides of her face. She threw herself into Alex's arms and held him for a long moment. Alex could tell she was trembling. "Oh, Alex, these last few minutes have been the worst of the whole trip. I saw you approach that man, then drive away with him and I had no idea where you were going or what would happen next. I half expected the KGB to come storming in here any minute."

"We're not very far ahead of them," Alex responded, "but I have transportation waiting and we've got to get out of here immediately." As Alex was speaking, Dr. Orgutsov appeared at the door. "Let's get out of here," Alex said. He motioned to Karen to leave her luggage as she started gathering it together. She managed to grab one small bag. Dr. Orgutsov had a small suitcase with him as well.

When they got to the lobby, Alex nodded to his new ally and taking the arms of his two companions, guided them through the door to the waiting Volga. "Mikhal insisted upon calling headquarters," the man said, indicating his fellow agent.

"That is all right," Alex replied. "What did he tell them?"

"That I am going with the three of you and will report on your destination. Colonel Zhukov has just now landed at the airport and is on his way here now."

"Good. You can come back here and get him when the time is right. That will give me time to accomplish my mission." These words were spoken at the rear of the car while putting the luggage in the trunk. Alex smiled at the fact the young agent had carefully avoided talking where the two "dissidents" could overhear him. The four climbed into the little car and Alex gave directions to the collective farm north of town.

Sitting in the rear seat, Karen couldn't help but marvel at Alex's boldness. No wonder he had been successful as a CAFI agent. He had walked right up to an enemy agent deep within Communist Russia, and within a short time that agent was helping them escape. Karen had no idea what Alex had told the man and she couldn't wait to ask. Orgutsov seemed lost in his own thoughts. No doubt his emotions were a combination of fear and excitement: Fear of the unknown, fear of flying in the Eagle, fear of what he would discover in America, fear of being caught trying to leave his own country.

While making their way through the city to the road which would take them north to the wheat farm and the abandoned airport, Alex knew he had to keep the driver's mind involved. He had to make sure the young agent would not have time to wonder at the present direction of events—events in which he seemed to be caught up unwittingly—and decide he had been duped. Alex kept the man occupied by making small talk and by giving directions in such a way the man had to be alert for the next turn. He was careful not to ask Alex anything that would give away his mission to the two adversaries in the back seat. Alex could tell, however, he was anxious to have the details filled in and was very concerned about doing the right thing as far as his superiors were concerned.

In order to successfully use him, Alex had to take advantage of the built-in fears which were part of any police official's life within the U.S.S.R. The man's career was totally based upon his successes and failures in the eyes of his immediate superior and how successful he was able to make that superior look to those in authority over him. So far, Alex had succeeded in making the man feel he was part of something important that would make his boss in the GRU look good compared to the KGB Colonel Zhukov. When they got to the abandoned airport, Alex would have to remain equally convincing in order to get the man to leave them there.

Alex had the young agent drive them to a spot directly in front of an abandoned hangar two buildings away from the one in which the Eagle was stored. As the car stopped, he jumped out with the driver, telling the other two to remain seated for a moment. Meeting the Russian at the rear of the car, Alex quickly gave him instructions. "The meeting is to be held here in approximately one hour. That will give you time to return to the hotel and bring Zhukov here. If you possibly can, bring your immediate superior with you. He will know who I am once he learns the details of my mission here and can assist me in seeing our organization gets the credit for this victory instead of the self-serving KGB colonel, Zhukov. We will be in this building when you return. I recommend you surround it from the outside and when you show yourselves, do so quickly in order to maintain the element of surprise. These people are not armed, however, some of the others may be, so be careful."

After removing the bags from the trunk of the Volga, Alex motioned Karen and Dr. Orgutsov toward the old hangar building and stood away from the car as the Soviet agent departed. As soon as the car was out of sight, Alex ran toward the building where the Eagle was stored, motioning for the other two to join him. They should have plenty of time to become airborne before the others returned. Fortunately, Grant Sopin was nowhere in sight.

20

Zhukov arrived at the hotel near the center of Magadan only to discover the two Americans and their Soviet traveling companion had just left for a destination unknown. The fact their driver was a GRU agent did not comfort him one bit. Zhukov was now convinced it was Alex Davis he was chasing, and knowing Davis' ability to devise schemes to impede his discovery and capture, he was furious the GRU had been taken in. He was convinced Davis had duped the unsuspecting agents into helping him escape.

Anxious to do something, but having no idea of where to begin his search, he compensated by taking his wrath out upon the agent, Mikhal, who had remained behind. Mikhal tried to explain to the fuming KGB colonel his companion would return shortly and take them to the ones they sought, but Zhukov was not convinced that was the case. He was on the phone to GRU headquarters, insisting all available personnel, including the local police, be pressed into a search for the Volga.

The local GRU commander, Major Georgi Murzin, left his office to meet Colonel Zhukov at the hotel. He was disturbed by the commotion being caused by this KGB officer. To him the assignment, called in through channels, had been a routine one, in which three people who were only suspected to be engaged in some dissident activities were to be watched and their activities reported on. There had been no indication the KGB in Moscow was interested in these three and there was a high-ranking KGB official on their tail. If his field agents had truly made a critical mistake, he could have been done in without having even known about it.

Murzin arrived at the hotel just as the agent who had taken Alex and his companions to the collective farm, drove up. There was much hurried conversation and the three available cars were loaded, amidst a lot of confusion and impatience. They raced off in pursuit of the three fugitives. Mikhal's companion didn't know whether he was a hero or villain. He hoped the GRU agent would be there with the two dissidents and the other anti-Soviet sympathizers with whom they were meeting. If so, he would truly have lucked into a major accomplishment. If they were gone … well, he didn't even want to think about that possibility.

21

J. L. McDaniels called Susan Davis from his office in San Antonio. "Susan, can you meet me in Houston this evening to catch a Wein Air Alaska flight to Nome?" he queried. "If my interpretation of the information I am currently receiving is correct, Alex will be there sometime tomorrow. He should be glad to see us."

"Yes, of course," Susan answered. "Where and when do I meet you?" She searched the drawer in the bedside table for a pen or pencil as McDaniels gave her the information. As soon as she had the details, she hung up. Picking up the phone again, she called the airlines. McDaniels had seemed confident they would see Alex. She hoped he was all right and Karen was too. Funny, she thought, I didn't even to think to ask if Karen really was with Alex after all.

22

Running quickly up to the hangar door, Alex slid it open and stepped inside. The Eagle was gone! In fact, the whole building was empty! Impossible! Where was the plane?

Alex ran back outside to be certain he had the right building. He was sure, but he checked the almost identical looking buildings on either side just to be positive. Each of them was empty as well. When Alex had been there before, they had all been filled with wheat.

Time was running out! Alex had allowed forty-five minutes to an hour for the GRU agent to return to the hotel and bring Zhukov to the farm. By then, he planned to have been airborne for at least half an hour. With the Eagle's disappearance went their only means of escape. Looking around, Alex noticed the tractors that had been on the end of the runway were gone as well. He had to find Grant Sopin to find out what had happened, but it would burn up precious time for him to walk to the farm headquarters. Instructing Karen and Dr. Orgutsov to check the remainder of the buildings, then to wait for him in the woods behind the row of hangars, Alex set off at a jog toward the building where he had first met the young farmer.

Grant was not in the house. Neither was the truck in sight. In fact, the entire farm looked quite deserted. Alex looked around defeated. He started walking back toward the row of hangars, trying to catch his breath. The jog had almost done him in. His physical conditioning was far from what it should have been for a mission like this. Alex began to realize how utterly foolish it had been for him to even begin such an undertaking. Then he shook those thoughts out of his head. Karen was with him and she would be depending upon him to get her out of this mess. He had to find that plane. Then, from behind him, Alex heard the farm truck drive up. He turned around to see Grant Sopin's smiling face.

"Major Korbut," Grant called. "I was beginning to wonder if you were ever coming back for your plane."

"Where is it, Grant?" Alex inquired impatiently as he ran up to him. "I have to leave immediately."

"Sure, I will take you to it. Get in." Alex and Grant climbed into the two and a half ton farm truck and Grant turned it back toward the main road.

"Wait, Grant. I have some people with me. They are near where I left the plane and we need to pick them up."

"Yes, sir," Grant replied, obviously wondering at this turn of events. "Does this mean I do not get my ride?"

Alex hesitated a minute before answering. "Grant, you can have your ride, but there is something about it you will need to know before deciding whether or not you really want it. For reasons I cannot explain right now, I can only tell you the details just before we are airborne." That seemed to satisfy the farmer for the time being. He started explaining why the Eagle was missing as he turned back around and headed for the abandoned airfield.

"The day after you left, I got a call the trucks were coming to remove the wheat stored in all of the barns. I knew you did not want the airplane discovered, so I took the liberty of moving it to another hiding place."

Alex was relieved. "Where did you hide it, Grant? How did you get it there," he asked.

"I moved the plane to an equipment storage shed located approximately two kilometers down the road. There are several combines parked around it so it would not be immediately visible to anyone passing by," Grant told him.

Then he continued, "Major Alexi Korbut, I have thought often during the days and nights since you left here that you are not who or what you claim to be. I am not certain why I feel this way, and I admit the feeling has come and gone, but nevertheless the doubts have been there. Whoever you are, there are two things I do know about you: One is you are a good person. The other is you managed to bring a little excitement into this farmer's dull life. For these two reasons I decided to help you." Then he smiled broadly. "Actually, there is another reason. I did not want to explain to the foreman of this collective farm why it is I allowed an airplane to be hidden in one of the wheat holding barns."

"Yes," Alex replied, "I can see what you mean. How did you move the airplane?"

"Well, I figured the plane must roll quite easily since you had been able to push it into the wheat barn by yourself. I tried it, and indeed I could move it, finding the wheels turned freely. I pulled it outside and hooked a chain to a ring attached to the bottom of the aircraft, near its tail. I then hooked the chain to a tractor and towed the plane to the shed. I did this at night so no one would see. The way is very open, so the wings gave me no problem."

"Very clever of you," Alex commented. Grant seemed pleased. Meanwhile, they had driven up to the hangar. Alex stepped out and called for Karen and Dr. Orgutsov, who quickly ran out of the woods toward the waiting truck. Since there was very little room in the cab, Alex motioned for Karen and the doctor to get in with Grant while he stood on the running board. After hasty introductions, first name only, Grant started the truck and drove to the spot where the Eagle was hidden. Alex surveyed the route from the truck's running board. He would be able to taxi the Eagle along the farm road, but he would not be able to take off until he got back to the abandoned runway. The plane would be heavily loaded and would need lots of concrete to obtain the speed necessary to become airborne. As Grant pulled up beside the shed, Alex began barking orders.

"Grant, you and Karen move the combines while I check the airplane." The fact Karen had grown up on Tennessee farm had given her a familiarity with farm machinery which had never left her. In fact, unlike many women, she was comfortable with almost any type of machinery. She climbed aboard the nearest diesel combine as Grant stopped with her just long enough to point out the starter switch. He ran over and climbed aboard the second combine that was blocking the Eagle's way as Karen began starting the big machine.

While the two of them were thus engaged, Alex was getting Dr. Orgutsov into the back seat of the Eagle. There was both fear and hesitation on the doctor's face. Alex wished Karen had brought her medical supplies so she could give the Soviet doctor something that would enable him to relax. His fear might pose a problem.

Strapping the doctor into the back seat, Alex turned his attention to the instrument panel in front of him. He wanted to drain some fuel from each of the airplane's sump tanks to free the fuel supply from water or other contaminants. He gave up the idea, hoping the long taxi back to the airfield would be sufficient to insure the engine was getting good fuel before the plane became airborne.

Flipping switches, Alex started the engine and checked the gauges. He was just turning on the radio equipment, including the UHF radio and the disponder when Karen and Grant approached the plane. They had cleared a path sufficient for the Eagle to taxi.

Grant helped Karen up onto the wing, then climbed up himself as she was fastening her seatbelt in the right-hand front seat of the plane. Leaning over Karen, Grant looked to Alex for an explanation. He was holding the door open against the prop blast of the idling engine and was straining to hear over the engine noise.

"Grant," Alex began, "This flight is going to terminate in America. I fully intended to take you on an airplane ride before I had to leave, but under the present circumstances, I can only take you if you are willing to go the entire route. These two people with me are physicians—one American and one Soviet. Together they have the ability to cure people of cancer. We feel the best chance for that cure to be developed is within the United States. There are others within your government who feel otherwise. In fact, KGB agents will be arriving back at the deserted airfield any minute now to try to stop us from leaving. If you remain out of sight until they are gone, it is possible you will not be implicated. If you wish to go with us, there is no turning back."

Grant seemed to weigh the alternatives. Alex had weighed the possibility that going to America might appeal to Grant before making his speech. The truth of the matter was the added weight would be detrimental to them and could possibly affect the successful outcome of the flight. He hoped the young farmer would decide not to go, but on the other hand, the opportunities within his country were severely limited according to what the man would find in America. Finally, Grant smiled. "This time, I must say no. There is family to consider. But if you were ever to come again, perhaps my answer would be different. Who knows? Now, you must get out of here. Good luck."

As Grant stepped down from the wing, Alex waited for him to move away from the prop blast, then gunned the engine. The farm road was dusty and rough and Alex was only able to taxi as fast as a man could run. The two kilometers between their present location and the runway seemed endless.

Zhukov and the others drove up to the empty hangar just as Alex began taxiing almost a mile away. They quickly surrounded the building, as had been suggested, and Zhukov boldly threw open the door. He stood in the doorway with his pistol drawn and armed men on either side of him. The hangar was empty. Disgusted, he turned to the GRU agent who had led them there and yelled, "You fool! Where are they?" Turning to the man's commander, Major Murzin, Zhukov shook his fist. "If they are gone, Comrade, I will hold you personally responsible." He gave orders for the men to spread out quickly and to check the remaining hangars.

At first, the sound of the taxiing plane had been noticed by Zhukov, Murzin or any of the other men searching for the missing three. They had subconsciously passed it off as a piece of farm equipment, nothing unusual for this area. It was Dmitri Flerov, standing beside Zhukov, who pointed out the approaching dust cloud, wondering what it was. It certainly did not seem like a tractor. As the shape materialized into that of an airplane, the Russians immediately began running toward their cars. Zhukov screamed at his driver to stop them before they became airborne. Foolishly, the man drove toward the area the plane was just approaching. Had he known anything at all about airplanes, he would have headed for an intercept point somewhere down the runway, a point in which he would have the opportunity to obstruct the aircraft before it reached takeoff speed.

When Alex reached the concrete, he saw the commotion near the hangars and the cars starting toward him. The aircraft was headed downwind, a condition which would considerably lengthen their takeoff roll and make it more difficult to get airborne. Had he been given the time, Alex would have taxied to the far end of the runway and taken off in the direction from which they were now traveling. As he opened the throttle, Karen was leaning over her seat attending to Dr. Orgutsov, who appeared as if he were about to pass out. Not knowing his physical condition, Karen feared a heart attack. She was trying to loosen the doctor's collar and at the same time, open her window slightly in order to get him some air.

She heard a thud as a bullet struck the plane. It had been fired from one of the cars approaching from Alex's side of the aircraft. They had no idea where the bullet had hit the Eagle, but the engine was still producing full rpm and the plane was approaching flying speed. Two of the cars sped alongside the runway, their passengers firing pistols at the departing Eagle. Down the way, a third car stopped and one of the passengers got out with a rifle. Alex knew that could present a real problem if the plane could not become airborne before it reached the rifleman. The airspeed indicator was fluctuating just below liftoff speed. A bullet in either the engine, a fuel tank or one of the tires would be disastrous. Fortunately, the accuracy of those firing pistols from moving cars suffered. The man with the rifle, however, would be a different story altogether.

Alex eased back on the yoke and the Eagle struggled into the air. As soon as it broke ground Alex flipped the switch that raised the landing gear, thereby decreasing drag on the airframe. Lowering the nose to pick up flying speed, he made a ninety degree right turn, just as the man with the rifle took aim. Climbing for altitude, Alex jerked the airplane spasmodically through a series of turns. It wouldn't do anything for Orgutsov's fear of flying, but at the moment Alex was more concerned with making the aircraft a difficult target for the men below, especially the one with the rifle.

As the Eagle climbed out of sight over the mountains northeast of Magadan, Colonel Zhukov could not believe what he was seeing. Surely the arrogant Alex Davis did not think he could escape the entire Soviet Air Force in a single-engine propeller plane. As soon as they had determined the direction in which the Eagle was headed, Zhukov had his driver take him to a phone. On the way, he was thinking about the American movie *Firefox*, and how Davis probably got his ideas from such a movie. That was all right. The airplane he had just seen was no MIG and the Soviet Air Force would blow it right out of the sky.

Within ten minutes, they pulled up outside a police building and Zhukov called KGB headquarters. Briefly, he explained the situation and requested a patch into the Soviet Air Defense Command. When he had the strike commander on the phone, he relayed the circumstances.

"General Marchenko, as you know by now, an American airplane departed from a deserted airfield north of the city of Magadan with a Soviet citizen and two Americans aboard. Their destination is unknown, but presumably it is the United States. To let them get out of this country would be an embarrassment to both the military and the KGB."

"Calm down, Colonel Zhukov," Marchenko replied. "They will not reach American soil. However, none of my radar stations have reported such an unidentified aircraft. Are you certain?"

"Comrade General, I saw it myself!" Zhukov insisted.

"It is headed northeast, you say?" the General asked. "It would seem to me the most expedient way to get out of our country would be across the Sea of Okhotsk to Japan."

"That may be, Comrade General, and they may turn that way, but they were headed over the mountains when I last saw them," Zhukov said.

"We are scrambling the intercept squadrons from Magadan and from Chabarovsk to have a look. If he is out there, even over the water, we will find him."

"You had better, Comrade General Marchenko," Zhukov fumed. Then in a more conciliatory tone asked, "Where can I monitor the proceedings? If there is a possibility of forcing the plane down rather than destroying it, I would like to get my hands on the man who is flying it."

"I understand, Comrade Colonel Zhukov. You can best follow the action from the radar room at Magadan Airport. The Air Force section is entered from the west side of the airport. I will inform the facility commander to expect you."

General Marchenko was disgusted with the pompousness of the KGB Colonel. Did the man think an American civil aircraft was a match for their Soviet MIGs? He had obtained a brief description of the airplane just as Zhukov's call was being patched in to him. According to what Zhukov had told the communications center, the aircraft was a single-engine, propeller-driven plane. They should have both radar and visual sightings within just a few minutes. Then that plane would be history.

Alex had Karen scanning the UHF channels, listening for any sign of MIG squadrons that would be looking for them.

He had turned the disponder on in the standby position, which meant it was warmed up and ready to go, but not transmitting any signals. The plane would be invisible to any ground radar stations without the disponder. It might be possible for them to make it all the way back to Alaska without using the disponder at all, but that was something yet to be determined.

Dr. Orgutsov, in the back seat, was obviously tense, as Karen observed the whites of his knuckles where he gripped the edge of his seat. He was looking straight ahead in a fixed stare. There was no possibility he would be of any use in helping them to spot any planes which might approach them.

Early in his planning, Alex had considered flying to Japan when they left Russia. The distance would be much shorter, but there would be major obstacles to overcome. He didn't think he would find the Japanese authorities very cooperative if he dropped in unannounced, and he didn't have any contacts in the government who could help him. Heading for Japan would have had him out of Soviet airspace within thirty minutes. Even then, the Russians would probably pursue him far out into the Sea of Okhotsk with fighters from both Khabarovsk and the Kamchatka Peninsula. For these reasons, he had decided to fly all the way back to Alaska, following much of the same route over which he had come before. This would put them over Soviet airspace for approximately seven hours. The Windecker would, in effect, be running a gauntlet the entire time. Zhukov would stop at nothing in an attempt to bring Alex and his passengers down. Alex hoped the Soviet Air Force would give up after several hours of not being able to locate the plane. In three more hours it would be dark. The darkness would be an ally.

Zhukov arrived in the radar room at Magadan Airport just as the first visual sighting was called in. It had not been one of the MIGs that had spotted the Eagle, but a ground watch station near Palana on the Kamchatka Peninsula. The aircraft had been spotted crossing the bay at approximately 7,000 feet, still heading northeast. Zhukov turned to the station commander who was ordering a flight of interceptors into that area.

"Why do we not have him on radar, Commander?" Zhukov wanted to know.

"I do not know, Comrade Colonel. All of our fighters are visible on the radar screen. The enemy airplane should present a small, but identifiable target. We will have him soon. Then our MIGs will be able to close in on him. We have calculated his groundspeed to be less than 325 kilometers per hour. He will be no match for our jets. Also, we have ascertained he has not set his course for Japan, but continues to head Northeast."

The station commander was calm and confident. It was obvious to Zhukov he considered this a simple exercise, one that would easily be successfully completed. The man had no idea what kind of adversary he was up against, or he would not be so confident. Zhukov would not have been surprised if Alex Davis had walked up and taken charge of the mission, so brazen was the man.

"Move all of your MIGs into that area!" barked Zhukov. "Saturate the airspace. Give him no empty sky in which to fly."

"I am not sure that would be wise, Comrade Colonel Zhukov," replied the commander. "The sighting was not positive and we still do not have radar identification. We must continue to cover all contingencies."

In the Eagle, Karen had finally stumbled across the UHF frequency the Soviets were using for their primary air-to-ground communications. They heard the MIGs being deployed toward the peninsula beyond Palana and Alex knew his American plane had been spotted. It was time to give the Russians a target. He turned the disponder on, but not before setting a displacement that would show the Eagle to be two hundred miles south of its actual location.

The excitement in the radar room was hard to contain. "We have him, Comrade Commander," shouted one of the radar operators. "The stupid fool has turned his transponder on and is transmitting a signal."

"Good work, Comrade," the commander replied. "Give the two lead flights vectors to the area. Bring flights three and four around on an intercept heading in case the first flights miss his altitude."

"Yes, sir," the radar operator responded. Colonel Zhukov and the commander went over to the radar screen and watched over the operator's shoulder. Flerov was standing away from the action, secretly hoping his commander would fail and he would be given an opportunity to oppose the American. It was obvious to Flerov that Zhukov overrated the man. Capturing him should be a piece of cake. He was anxious to find out where the Soviet Air Force would force Davis to land. He wanted to be there.

In the Eagle, Alex heard directions being given to the MIG flight commanders as they were sent to the phony location indicated by the disponder. Right away, he knew he had made a mistake by displacing the signal too far. Someone in the command center would pick up on the fact it should have taken an hour for the plane to have spanned the distance from the visual sighting to the place where radar identification had been made. A better move would have been a slight displacement in which the separation continued to grow. It was too late for that now.

The displaced signal would parallel the Eagle's actual course. If the MIGs continued to search that area long enough, Alex would be able to take refuge in the eastern Siberian mountains and the oncoming darkness. He had chosen his present altitude to minimize the noise level which could be distinguished from the ground until he could get to more sparsely populated territory. The winds at that altitude were in his favor, also, giving the Eagle a tailwind.

Listening to the radio, Alex heard the MIG pilots set up a search pattern that would sweep the area of the radar signal. They were staggering their altitudes wisely. A visual sighting was expected any minute. Several of the MIGs reported picking up the signal on their airborne radar and were closing in for the kill.

In the radar room, Zhukov was pacing. He did not want Davis shot down, but wanted him forced back to Magadan. He wanted the American to know once and for all by whom he had been defeated. "Order those planes not to shoot the American down," Zhukov told the commander. "Have them force him to land here."

"That's all very well, Colonel Zhukov," the commander replied, "but right now they should have visual contact and they do not. I am still concerned about the visual sighting to the north. Either that was not the American, or this is not. It is physically impossible for the plane to be in both locations."

"What do you mean, Comrade?" Zhukov queried.

"I mean I suspect a trick, Colonel."

"Impossible!" Zhukov insisted. "Radar doesn't lie, does it?"

"Generally not, Colonel Zhukov, but something is wrong," the general answered.

Alex gave the MIG pilots and radar operators a few minutes to become thoroughly confused, then he turned the transponder back to standby, causing the signal to disappear. That action resulted in a lot of chatter between the ground units and the Soviet jets. Clearly the Russians were confused as to what action to take next.

Meanwhile, the Eagle crossed over a small mountain range and Alex descended into the Anadyr Valley. He planned to follow the Anadyr River eastward toward the Gulf. By flying below the mountain ridges in this sparsely populated area, he should stay below the search altitude of any fighters that might be directed this way. The Eagle would blend in with the earth below, making it even more difficult for the higher flying MIGs to locate him visually. Inside the American-made aircraft, the time seemed to expand into eternity. There were no navigation radio stations for Alex to tune in that would enable him to get an actual fix on his location and to determine the groundspeed at which they were traveling. Alex guessed it to be close to 200 knots, but the expansive country below made it seem as if they were barely moving.

Now that Alex had been able to stabilize his flight path, keeping the wings level and avoiding any abrupt maneuvers, Dr. Orgutsov was beginning to relax. He and Alex engaged in some interesting conversations as the doctor began to ask Alex how he had come to be so familiar with the Soviet language, customs and geography. Alex started telling the doctor of his background and of the time he had spent behind the Iron Curtain. Karen tried to follow the conversation, but her grasp of the Russian language was still in its infancy stage and she found she was only able to pick up bits and pieces of the story Alex was telling.

He was a strange mixture of candor and mystery, this brother of hers. The strength of their friendship throughout the years had been Alex's openness with her and hers with him. She couldn't believe he had ever hidden anything from her during the entire thirty years she had known him. Yet his very existence within the CAFI organization had been based upon secrecy. Such a strange combination to be rolled up in one character—this tendency to be an open book to those he loved, yet a master at disguise and deception in his professional life.

As Karen observed these thoughts now, flying over the desolate Siberian countryside and listening to her friend, she couldn't help but wonder if Alex's purpose in being so open with Lev Orgutsov was to gain his confidence and set him at ease. It seemed to be something Alex knew how to do well. To gain someone's respect, you must be as you appear to be. That was Alex's definition of integrity. He did not define integrity as being above reproach, but rather being transparent. Orgutsov seemed to be more at ease, now that Alex was reassuring him.

Karen determined to apply herself diligently to mastering the Russian doctor's native language. She looked forward to working closely with him as he refined his medical procedure and taught it to the American experts who would make the cure widely known. For Karen, there would be many rewarding days ahead.

Alex didn't have a map which covered anything west of the Russian city of Anadyr, so there was not much he could do to navigate except to follow the river and keep track of the time. The chatter on the UHF radio continued, but with no positive direction. Alex turned the volume down, subconsciously listening for anything significant. This act was typical of most pilots who are accustomed to tuning out irrelevant radio noise. As the afternoon wore on, Alex found himself growing sleepy. Looking over at Karen, he observed her nodding off to sleep also, lulled by the drone of the engine and the barrenness of the landscape below them.

Suddenly the voices on the radio were filled with excitement. Alex leaned forward and turned up the radio volume. Suddenly, he saw they were flying head-on toward a helicopter! He recognized it immediately as an MI-14 Haze, a turbine-powered helicopter the Soviet Navy Air Wing used for electronic surveillance and for submarine spotting. There was no doubt the Haze pilot had spotted the Eagle. In fact, he had probably been looking for them.

Alex dove for the deck, pushing the Eagle's airspeed far into the caution range. The Haze pilot also turned quickly and followed Alex down toward the river. Alex had a slight speed advantage over the helicopter, but the Haze made up for some of the difference by being highly maneuverable. For a long ten minutes, the race was a battle of pilot skills as Alex sought to outrun the Soviet helicopter and to seek refuge among the surrounding mountains. As the Soviet helicopter fell behind, its pilot climbed for altitude to try to gain visual advantage.

Alex estimated darkness to be still over an hour away. He had no idea what type of electronic tracking equipment the helicopter had on board, but he was certain it was pretty sophisticated. As soon as he had a free moment to turn his attention toward it, Alex turned on the disponder and set it to produce multiple signals. The Haze would have MIGs on the way and Alex would have a tough time avoiding their missiles if they ever locked onto him.

His first thoughts were to stay low and seek cover among the draws and valleys of the surrounding mountains, but as he crossed a ridgeline on a northerly heading, Alex encountered a layer of stratus clouds. Climbing inside the cloud layer, Alex sought an altitude that would keep him free of any mountain peaks that might be reaching up unsuspectingly from below. While still heading north, he adjusted the three phantom radar signals to roughly parallel his course. He set one target 50 miles to his left side, one 25 miles to his right side, and one 30 miles behind him. As soon as the signals were transmitting steadily, Alex turned the Eagle toward the East. The phantom signals would turn as well, for the one limitation they had was they would always maintain a constant relationship from the host unit. The only way to change the relative location was to adjust the radial and distance settings on the disponder control head. Alex pointed out the switch settings to Karen and instructed her to randomly change the pattern in order to keep the Soviets guessing. Meanwhile, there was the remote possibility the Haze's electronics were sophisticated enough to pick up the raw return from the Eagle's skin. Alex didn't see how that was possible, but the pilot had located him once. Whether by luck or technology, Alex didn't know for certain.

When the helicopter pilot reported he had spotted the Eagle, Zhukov was both relieved and ecstatic. He had really stuck his neck out by ordering the Navy task force to deploy its helicopter ECM squadron up the Anadyr River. It had been a long shot, but one that had paid off. After the signal over the water had disappeared and the MIGs had abandoned their search in that area, Zhukov had stood before the large wall map in the operations room and studied it carefully. Flerov had joined him there and the two of them had apparently been thinking the same thing.

They plotted a course line from Magadan to the location of the visual sighting near Palana. Then they followed the natural course of the terrain a pilot might take if he wanted to avoid extended flight over the icy waters of the Bering Sea. The obvious natural navigation aid was the Anadyr River. The helicopter that had chanced upon Alex had been one of eighteen such helicopters flying up that valley at staggered altitudes. Even now the remaining helicopters were joining the search, but they would not be able to stay on station but fifteen to twenty minutes longer before they would have to return to their home base for fuel.

After the sighting, Dmitri Flerov quietly slipped out of the operations room and headed toward the flight line. The MIGs that were stationed at Magadan were all participating in the search for the American Aircraft. Groups of these MIGs were landing at the base periodically to refuel. Now that the enemy had been spotted in the Anadyr Valley, recently refueled aircraft would be joining the chase. By brandishing his identification in front of the officer in charge of flight operations, Flerov was able to procure a ride in a two-seat MIG that would be taking off momentarily. The aircraft would be one of four in a flight that would fly directly to the sight where the Eagle was last seen and attempt to locate it with the help of whatever helicopters were still on station. When the Eagle was confronted by the MIGs, its pilot would be forced to land at Anadyr. Flerov intended to be there.

It was to Zhukov's disadvantage he thought of the same thing ten minutes too late. The aircraft had all departed. He was not aware Flerov was aboard one of them until thirty minutes later when he chanced to overhear a conversation on the radio about a KGB officer who was flying with one of the interceptor pilots. The KGB Colonel was furious.

The clouds were thinning and Alex was getting worried. He was unaware of the other helicopters because they were operating on a frequency other than the one the Air Force had been using. He was aware, however, of a number of MIGs heading his way. From what he could determine, there were at least two flights of MIG 25 Foxbats, and two flights of MIG 31 Foxhounds enroute. That would mean eight of the high performance interceptors would be zeroing in on him. Finding him would be like finding a needle in a haystack, but that was the job these pilots were trained for and they would be good at it. Alex would have to play his two primary advantages: his radar invisibility as a primary target and the deceptive capabilities of the disponder, for all they were worth.

In the Central Air Defense Command Center, located in Moscow, a perceptive computer operator was onto something. He was making some calculations based on information being relayed to him via high speed communications. The radar patterns of the activity in eastern Siberia were being duplicated on the scope in front of him. The phantom signals the pursued aircraft seemed to be producing were being automatically fed into the computer. The technician at the console had a theory. Never had there been any indication there was more than one aircraft, yet multiple targets continued to appear on the radar scope. The discreet signal each of these targets was producing transmitted the same code as the other two. The only way this could be true would be if there was one signal somehow being electronically multiplied and displaced. If that were the case, there would be a formula that could be calculated which would indicate the location of the unit producing the signals. The technician was so confident he would be able to calculate the relative location of the aircraft from these phantom signals, he shared his theory with his supervisor. The supervisor immediately transferred the signals to two other stations and put those technicians on the problem as well. They were racing the clock. It would soon be dark in the East and if the pilot turned off that signal, they might never locate him in the darkness.

Alex continued to listen to the MIG pilots as they flew their search patterns near the Eagle's flight path. The radar signals the disponder was generating were obviously fooling the Soviet pilots, but it made them more determined than ever to make a visual sighting. The layer of cloud he had been using for cover was all but gone now, so Alex turned off the disponder's multiple signal mode and began descending. He was no longer in the Anadyr Valley, but a few miles north in unfamiliar country.

With the darkness approaching, Alex found himself using the mountains for cover. The area was largely unsettled and the absence of lights on the ground made the darkness seem to swallow the Eagle into a dark vacuum. Alex wanted to find a pass through the mountains which would allow him to turn back toward the Anadyr Valley, but so far none had appeared. He knew he could continue eastward from his current location and eventually hit the Alaskan coast, but the magnetic variation in this far north country affected his compass so much, Alex wanted to align his course with landmarks he recognized before crossing the Bering Strait. The radio frequency they were monitoring was filled with sounds of MIG pilots searching, but so far they had been unable to locate a frequency being used by the helicopters. Whether the choppers were still in the chase or not, Alex did not know.

Alex had Karen and Dr. Orgutsov helping him keep watch for rapid changes in the terrain. The last thing they needed now was a collision with the side of a mountain. The moon would be of some help. It was nearly full, but a layer of high cirrus clouds obscured it from view at times. When the moon was visible, its light was useful in helping Alex to pick out landmarks on the ground.

The MIG Dmitri Flerov had boarded in Magadan was now part of a task force that had just received some updated information concerning the American aircraft. The MIG pilots were acting upon this information with some degree of anticipation. Just before Alex had switched the disponder from the multiple signal mode, the computer operator in Moscow had pinpointed what he believed to be the exact location of the Eagle. The operators at the other two consoles had quickly verified the figures, and the message had been passed to the Russian pilots who were involved in the search. The computer had tracked the Eagle and was now plotting the projected course based on its last fifteen minutes of travel. The Soviet Air Defense Command suspected the American might be listening on their frequencies. For this reason, they continued to use the open frequencies for numerous aircraft while quietly switching the planes that were acting upon this new information to a discreet frequency. The radio signals on this new frequency were being scrambled. Alex's radio could not pick up these broadcasts even if he had been monitoring the correct frequency.

Having no knowledge of the American pilot's altitude, the four MIGs arrived in the area at a high altitude and began descending one at a time in a race track search pattern. Relying on input from Moscow via the scrambled signals, they were constantly altering their course to match the computer's projections of the most likely flight paths the American would be taking. If they were lucky, one of them would get a visual sighting during one of the moon's excursions from behind the clouds.

Far below in the darkness, another serious problem was developing that demanded Alex's attention. Just before running one of his wing tanks dry, he switched the selector to allow the engine to draw fuel from the other wing. Within seconds of making that switch, the engine began sputtering and threatening to quit. Immediately, Alex switched back to the original tank and the engine smoothed out again. The contamination Alex had feared in the Russian fuel was obviously the culprit. During the long flight, the sediment in the unused tank had settled to the bottom and was now blocking the fuel flow valve for the right wing tank. They had to have that fuel in order to make it home. The left tank and the auxiliary fuselage tank together held approximately thirty more minutes fuel at the most.

Alex had two options. One was to climb to a safe altitude, switch the tanks, and hope the engine could digest enough of the contaminated fuel to smooth out before he got too low. The other was to land and physically drain the sump pumps. In friendly terrain, the answer would have been a no-brainer. The second option would have been the only sensible solution. Even now, Alex was leaning that way. He had an aeronautical chart he had purchased in Alaska which covered the eastern part of the Asian continent. Anadyr was on that chart. Across the inlet from the city were two airports. One of them was a paved, lighted airport at the village of Leninka. That would be the airport used by Aeroflot and the military. The other was an unimproved strip used to supply fishermen. The chart indicated the strip was lit, but in such a remote area it should be deserted at night. They had just crossed a ridge that ran more or less north and south and below them was tundra. By turning southeast, Alex knew within the next twenty to thirty minutes they had a good chance of locating Anadyr and the two airports. He decided to climb just in case, but if he could safely land and drain the fuel sumps, he would feel much more secure crossing the icy waters of the Bering Strait.

The moonlight reflecting off the pools of water below helped Alex navigate. Unknown to him, the moonlight was also reflecting off the wing surfaces of the Windecker Eagle. High above the three unsuspecting passengers of the radar invisible plane, the Soviet KGB agent Dmitri Flerov considered himself a very fortunate man. Fate and the quick thinking that had caused him to seek a ride in the MIG had dealt him a rewarding victory. The American pilot's plane was clearly visible below. They now had only to force the American down. The MIG pilot wasn't being cooperative.

He, too, tasted the sweet savor of success, but his plane was running on fumes. He was landing at Anadyr before he and his passenger became entangled within the ball of metal the MIG would become if it didn't land within the next ten minutes. The pilot radioed the position of the Eagle to his command and supposedly the helicopters were on their way.

As they were leaving their station above the American, the young Soviet Air Force pilot made a comment to the KGB officer who was flying with him. He wondered why the American was flying toward Anadyr when a straight course toward Alaska would have taken them along the northern edge of the Gulf, not toward the city at all. The question puzzled Flerov and as he was pondering it, the MIG pilot added one more bit of intelligence. From what he could tell, the airplane was descending. These two items together led Dmitri Flerov to believe Davis intended to land near Anadyr. He inquired about landing sites and his pilot told him about the two possibilities.

"Why would he land now?" Flerov asked his pilot.

"Any number of reasons, Comrade," the pilot answered. "He could be having mechanical difficulties. He may have exhausted his fuel supply. Or he could be ill."

"Interesting," Flerov replied to the pilot. "But wouldn't he risk capture?"

"Not if he landed at Nerpichiy," the pilot answered. "He does not know we have sighted him and he does not know about the helicopters. Nerpichiy is a remote airstrip and one he would expect to be totally deserted at this time of night."

"Can we land at Nerpichiy?" Flerov wanted to know.

"Perhaps we could land safely, but the MIG would never be able to take off from there. It would have to be trucked out," the MIG pilot answered.

"Then do it," Flerov commanded.

"But, Comrade," the pilot enjoined, "It'll be my hide if I damage this airplane."

"I will take full responsibility. Now land at Nerpichiy."

The Soviet pilot just shrugged his shoulders and adjusted his course. He would be on the ground at Nerpichiy minutes before the American could get there, if that was where he was going. The pilot believed it was a long shot, but surely the American would not land at the larger airport twenty kilometers south at Leninka. Regardless of the outcome, he was ready to get his MIG on the ground. If the American did not arrive, he could always claim he had to make an emergency landing because he was out of fuel. That wasn't far from the truth, anyway.

Alex discussed his plan with Karen and Dr. Orgutsov. The two doctors, unused to being cramped up in a small aircraft, were ready to get out and stretch their legs anyway. Orgutsov agreed with Alex's theory there would most likely be no one around the small fishing village airport. Karen was more skeptical, but she didn't want to cross the Bering Strait with an engine that was struggling to stay alive. The three of them tightened their seatbelts and began searching the horizon for sign of the airport. Off to their right and slightly above them a jet, presumably a MIG, brushed past. He appeared to be descending to land at Leninka. Alex hoped the Eagle had not been spotted. Since he had no lights on and was making no radar target, it was very unlikely the pilot could have spotted them. Seeing the Kanchalan River below them, Alex turned to follow it. This river would lead them to the bay where they would find the airport on the northeast shoreline.

Zhukov was just arriving at Leninka. When the search had moved into the Anadyr area, he had caught a MIG flight directly to the air base at Leninka where he could be closer to the action. Now, walking into the operations building, he overheard the conversation between the controller and the pilot of the MIG in which Dmitri Flerov was a passenger. He was delighted the American plane had once again been sighted. As soon as he understood what Flerov was doing, Zhukov immediately ordered a helicopter to take him to the Nerpichiy airstrip. All of the helicopters were either airborne or refueling and Zhukov paced impatiently while one was being rerouted for him.

Alex and his passengers followed the river for fifteen minutes before they sighted the beacon marking the airstrip which they sought. Seeing no evidence of activity below, Alex set up for an approach to the airport.

"Karen," Alex said, "We will only be on the ground for five to ten minutes. You and Dr. Orgutsov get out and stretch your legs, or whatever you need to do while I drain the fuel, but you must get right back in and be ready to go. We cannot afford to hang around very long. Someone might hear us land and come to investigate."

"Sure," Karen answered, "But I need to find a bush and Lev probably could use a break, too."

"Okay, but make it quick," Alex replied.

The Eagle touched down smoothly and Alex allowed it to roll all the way to the end of the runway before stopping his engine. He turned the airplane so it was headed back down the runway in the direction from which they had just landed. There was very little wind on the ground, so it made no difference which way they made their takeoff. Alex wanted to be ready to go in a hurry. As soon as the propeller stopped, Karen opened the door on the right side of the Eagle and the three got out. Karen and Dr. Orgutsov went off in different directions to find a place to modestly relieve themselves, while Alex crawled under the fuselage and began to drain the sump pumps.

"Alex!" Karen's terrified yell split the otherwise silent night and caused a chill to go up Alex's spine. Quickly he climbed out from under the plane to find her.

"Hold it right there!" a voice said in Russian. Walking onto the edge of the tarmac, Alex could just make out the figure of Karen with a slim man, obviously not Orgutsov, behind her.

"Karen," Alex called softly, "What's wrong?"

"Silence, American," the Russian voice snapped at him. Alex breathed a sigh of relief. It was not Zhukov. It was then he saw the dark hulk of the MIG-25 looming in the shadows beside the runway. So, he *had* been spotted after all and the MIG occupants had done some quick thinking. It was time to try a bluff. Where was Orgutsov? Had he been sighted, or was he watching from the darkness, waiting for an opportunity to help? And was this the only occupant of the MIG, or was there another one nearby. This man was not dressed like a military pilot. Perhaps he had been a passenger in the MIG and the pilot was still about somewhere.

"You fool," Alex snapped. "Where is Zhukov? Does he know what you are doing?"

"Zhukov is not here," Flerov replied, "and this is one victory for which he will not get the credit."

"Look," Alex snapped in perfect Russian, "He worked too hard setting up this mission for you to blow it for him. Surely you're not here with his permission. He was supposed to meet me here himself and make the trip to America with me."

"What are you talking about?" Flerov asked. It was obvious he was beginning to wonder.

"Obviously you do not know who I am. You wouldn't unless you were Zhukov or Zhukov's number two man." Alex said.

"But I *am* Zhukov's number two. I am Dmitri Flerov, and you are Alex Davis, an American spy who is full of tricks, tricks I will not fall for. Now get your hands over your head and move over here where I can see you better."

"You're Flerov?" Alex queried. "But that's impossible. Zhukov originally set this mission up for Flerov. All of our preparations were made for Flerov until Zhukov decided to switch and take it himself. It is all set up for him to meet with the head of CAFI and he is supposed to be here now. If you were really Flerov, surely you would have been in on it."

Alex was buying time, hoping to come up with something. He could get the man wondering, but doubted if he could prod him into action unless a break came his way. Meanwhile, the absence of Dr. Orgutsov and the MIG pilot puzzled him. Alex could only control the situation if there were no unknowns. Right now he had two of them to worry about.

"What is this about meeting the head of CAFI? Surely Zhukov is not planning to defect?" Flerov said, with doubt in his voice.

"Not actually, but he certainly wants it to appear that way, at least he did for Flerov. You see, I am not Alex Davis. I am Colonel Grigori Kotosvk. Davis was killed a number of years ago, and I have been leading the life of a double agent since that time. To the Americans, I am Davis. To most Soviets, I am Davis. Zhukov and I have been working this angle for nearly ten years. He was to have one of his high ups, presumably you, appear to defect. I have it set up for that man to be accepted by the high authorities of CAFI as a genuine defector. Our plan is for that man to get to the head of CAFI, learn the entire operation, and then lead Soviet operatives within the United States in for the kill. If things go as we plan, that individual will return to the Soviet Union as a hero of the State."

While Alex was talking, he became aware of the approach of a helicopter, still some distance away. He also saw Lev Orgutsov standing behind Flerov with what appeared to be a large rock in his hand. As the sound of the helicopter grew louder, Flerov turned his attention to it.

"So," Alex commented, "Here is Zhukov arriving now. What an interesting situation he will discover. His number two man, if that's who you are, standing here, without orders, jeopardizing one of the most important missions of his entire career." Flerov looked toward the helicopter, looked at the Eagle, then looked at Alex. It was apparent he was puzzled about what to do. Alex knew that to say anything else would make him appear to be too eager. He had created the doubts in Flerov's mind and now the arrival of the helicopter was that perfect bit of good fortune needed to add credibility to Alex's accusations and to put pressure on Flerov to act.

Suddenly it was obvious Flerov had made up his mind. He had no doubts Zhukov was in the helicopter and he was coming there. Supposedly it was to capture Davis for himself, but who knew for sure what was going on. Suddenly the fourth seat in that American airplane seemed to have more promise, even if Davis or Kotosvk, whichever one he was, was lying, than having Zhukov arrive on the scene now and take all the credit for whatever happened.

"Quick," he said to Alex, "Let's get in your plane and get out of here." With that, he holstered the pistol he had been holding behind Karen's back and moved toward the door of the Windecker.

"Where's your pilot?" Alex called.

"At the far end of the field, in case you had landed in the opposite direction. He is probably halfway here by now, but it is a long walk."

Dr. Orgutsov threw down his rock and followed Flerov into the back seat of the plane. Alex got in the pilot's seat and Karen climbed into the front passenger seat. They shut the door and Alex started the engine just as the helicopter landed beside them. While it was still at a hover, Alex gunned his engine and went racing down the runway. The helicopter pilot accelerated also, his powerful turbine engines eager for the chase. Once airborne, Alex could outrun the helicopter, but here on the ground, the turbine-powered helicopter could keep pace with the Eagle.

Its pilot attempted to pull in front of Alex, but Alex turned sharply off the runway and the helicopter pilot had to lower his nose to accelerate again. The helicopter was highly maneuverable, but each time it got in front of Alex, it had to stop, and when Alex changed directions, he did so without reducing speed. The result was the Eagle continued to accelerate to its liftoff speed, even though not in a straight line, while the helicopter pilot was forced to stop and go in his attempt to force the Eagle to abort. Alex zipped around the helicopter and regained the runway surface. Ahead of him he saw a man, whom he presumed to be the MIG pilot, racing to get out of the way. Behind him the helicopter had once again turned and was bearing down on his plane. The Eagle broke ground and started climbing with the helicopter hot on his tail. The fuel load was light now, but the weight of the four adults in the plane could be felt. Alex knew he could outdistance the helicopter by flying straight and level, yet he had to gain some altitude to clear the dark terrain. In the climb, the helicopter had the advantage.

Alex turned north, then west, then south, in an effort to lose the helicopter in the darkness. Clearing a low ridgeline, he turned almost due east and as he did so, put the Eagle into a steep dive. He was headed for the tundra below and his increasing airspeed left the helicopter behind. Alex knew other aircraft would soon be joining the chase. He only hoped to put some distance between himself and the last position in which he had been sighted. Infrared search planes would be joining the search along with helicopters and jet interceptors. Zhukov would be throwing everything the Soviet Air Force had at him now after just missing them at Nerpichiy.

"Davis, what are you doing?" Zhukov's voice boomed over the UHF radio.

"It's all right, Veektor. Comrade Flerov is with me," Alex answered.

"Flerov! That imbecile!" Zhukov yelled. "I'll blow you out of the sky, you traitor!" Alex turned the radio volume down just as Flerov was starting to ask what he meant by that.

"Why does he not call off the search, Colonel Kotosvk?" Flerov asked.

"Oh, he's got to make it look good. Besides, if his plan was for him to be here instead of you, I think you have just made a formidable enemy, Comrade Flerov," Alex answered. "You had better be careful, when you return, that he doesn't sabotage your credibility."

Alex was now racing along just a few feet above the earth. The terrain beneath them was flat, nearly at sea level. There were still many miles to go before they would be back in Nome and it wasn't going to be easy evading capture as they crossed the remaining distance. The shortest route now would take them across the Gulf of Anadyr, but Alex ruled that out.

Highly sophisticated search planes would be monitoring the ice pack with infrared detecting equipment and they would be able to pick up the heat of the Eagle's engine in contrast to the ice. The alternative route would take them up north of the Gulf, and across 250 miles of mountainous terrain before they started across the strait.

By staying close to the terrain, Alex hoped to avoid detection by the MIGs and helicopters. He debated about using any of the disponder's capabilities and decided until there was evidence they were closing in on him, he would do better producing no signal at all. The terrain gradually increased to approximately 2,000 feet and Alex climbed accordingly. Hugging the now ragged terrain, the Windecker Eagle droned on toward the northeast at 160 knots indicated airspeed. Alex hoped there was still a tailwind.

In the helicopter, Zhukov anticipated Alex's hesitancy to cross the Gulf and had his pilot fly directly to a point near Velkal where Alex would have to cross a 40 kilometer stretch of water. The alternative was to fly another hundred kilometers north to go around it. The KGB Colonel radioed for other helicopters to join him there and for MIGs to provide high cover. The Eagle would present a visible target as it crossed the water.

It took forty-five minutes for Alex to reach the point where he intended to cross Zaliv Bay which jutted north out of the Gulf of Anadyr. Even though Veektor Zhukov had taken a more direct route, he had not yet arrived at that location. High overhead, two MIGs waited and as the Eagle turned to fly across the water, its silhouette became visible against the frigid waters below. Alex heard the MIG pilots report they had sighted him, and looking up, he spotted the two aircraft diving toward him. Heat-seeking missles would not be very effective against the composite structure of the Eagle. They would need a radar lock. He turned on the disponder, hoping to throw off the MIGs radar tracking.

Looking behind him, Alex saw the lights of a helicopter approach the point where he had started across the water. Guessing at the distance, Alex displaced the radar signal so it would approximate the location of the helicopter. Suddenly, two flashes appeared as the MIGs above and ahead of him fired their underwing missiles. The passengers of the Eagle watched as the missiles flashed past them and headed toward the helicopter. Within seconds, the helicopter exploded in a flash of light. Was it Zhukov? Alex had heard his voice on the radio just moments before the missiles had been fired. He didn't wait around to see. The MIGs had zoomed past him and and began a tight turn to try to pick him up again, Alex turned off his disponder and entered a cloud.

Inside the Eagle, Flerov was furious. Seeing the MIGs blow up the helicopter convinced him the man flying the airplane in which he was a passenger, actually *was* Davis and Davis had outwitted him. He drew his pistol, and pointing it at the back of Alex's head, ordered the American to land.

"Karen," Alex said, "You and Lev figure out some way to take care of this. We're starting to pick up ice on our wings and ahead of us there appears to be a snowstorm brewing. I've got my hands full flying this plane."

"Shut up and land this plane," Flerov commanded.

"I can't, you idiot. We'll all be killed if I try to turn around now. That was Zhukov in that helicopter back there. You think we're friends of the state after that?"

"You tricked me!" Flerov fumed.

"Alex, what's he saying?" Karen interrupted.

"He says we tricked him," Alex answered.

"You bet we did," Karen told the Russian. "And you'd better be glad we did. Don't you know what life in America is like? Listen, you don't have to answer to anybody like Zhukov. You can do what you want to do. You don't have to worry about somebody watching over your shoulder and breathing down your neck, just waiting to catch you at a mistake."

Flerov hesitated. He answered her in English, "What do you mean, I can do what I want to do? All of the good positions are handed down from generation to generation by the rich families who control your country."

"Bull," Karen answered, "Somebody's been lying to you. In our country you are limited only by your desire and how hard you are willing to work."

"But," Flerov continued, "I have a wife and a brother here, in the Soviet Union." He made this last statement to Dr. Orgutsov, once again speaking in his native language.

"Perhaps these two can get them out for you," Dr. Orgutsov volunteered. "They have certainly been resourceful in getting me out of bondage."

"We're not out yet, Doctor," Alex interrupted. "We've got troubles ahead."

"Don't say that, Mr. Davis," the Soviet doctor answered. "I was just beginning to get used to this flying business." He settled back in his seat as Karen smiled and reached for the gun Flerov was holding. Reluctantly, he handed it to her.

"It wouldn't be smart to shoot my pilot, would it Comrade Doctor? Especially when he might someday teach me to fly one of these machines." With that, Dmitri Flerov sat back in his seat to watch Alex deal with whatever crisis he was now facing.

What Alex was facing now was the weather. The Eagle's airframe was picking up a considerable load of ice because of the supercooled ice crystals from the cloud they were in. The ice added to the weight of the airframe and changed the shape of the wing so the stalling speed of the airplane was greatly increased. Any sudden maneuvering could cause the Eagle to stall. Up ahead was a full-blown snowstorm. The snow wouldn't add to the ice already on the airframe, but it would affect visibility and Alex's ability to navigate. There was one advantage: The snow would affect the visibility of the search aircraft as well.

Alex's last known location put him about 180 miles from the Russian coast, and another 120 miles from Nome. Normal flying speed would put them in Nome in about an hour and forty-five minutes. With the load of ice they were carrying, the flying time would be more than two hours *if* they could even maintain enough altitude to clear the mountain peaks ahead.

Alex held the Eagle on the fine edge of its flight envelope, a feat made more difficult by the fact he was flying solely by reference to the instruments on the panel in front of him. Maintaining the proper course without outside references was difficult due to the magnetic variation which affected the compass at this far north latitude. Even in the cool night air, Alex began to sweat. There had been a time, during his test pilot days, when his skills were more than adequate for this type of flying. Right now, he had his hands full.

"Karen," Alex said, "We have a problem."

"Oh, really?" Karen answered, tongue-in-cheek.

"I'm not talking about the ice or the snowstorm. I'm talking about the MIGs that will be waiting for us over the strait. They'll have every inch of the eastern coastline covered, just waiting for us to head out over the ice."

"Can we fool them and go north or south?" Karen asked.

"No, we can't," Alex responded. "I wish we could, but we don't have enough fuel. Besides, if I get too far off course, I might not find the Alaskan coastline."

"What do you think we should do?" she asked.

"I don't know," Alex said. "I'm thinking." The cockpit was quiet for a few minutes. The only sound was that of the engine. Karen started flipping the UHF channels, hoping to pick up some conversation from the pilots pursuing them. If Alex could determine their search pattern, perhaps he could think of a way to evade them.

Because of the snow, Alex could not track the Eagle's progress over the ground. He had no idea when they would leave the land and be over water. He would like to climb, thinking altitude would make it more difficult for infrared equipment to contrast his engine heat with the ice below. If the cloud cover continued over the strait, it would continue to provide concealment. Alex's weather experience told him not to expect low clouds over the water. The icy waters below would probably not be conducive to generating upper air disturbances on such a cool night.

Alex started a slow climb. It was possible he could find a temperature inversion that would melt the ice at some altitude. The climb was precarious and Alex stayed light on the controls, concentrating on his flying. The Eagle was no match for jet interceptors that would probably locate them crossing the strait. He had hoped to be well free from any pursuers by that time. The destruction of the helicopter had undoubtedly caused them to increase their efforts.

Slowly the plane staggered upward. As it went through 8,000 feet, the wings began shedding their ice. Gradually the Windecker's climb performance increased. Alex leveled off at 11,000 feet and tuned in the VOR station located near Nome. This radio navigation station would provide a signal that would indicate to Alex the direction he must fly in order to reach the Alaskan City. It was still too far away to get a strong signal, but the needle on the instrument panel was pointing in the general direction in which the city was located. They broke out on top of a layer of clouds. Fortunately, there was another layer above them which would help in their concealment. The airspeed trued out at just under 170 knots. Alex could now read the ground speed, and it showed to be approximately 210 knots. The night was dark, but beautiful.

The peace inside the aircraft was suddenly disturbed by the elevated sound of Russian voices on the UHF radio. They were onto something. To distract them, Alex turned on the disponder and set up six displacement locations, something that had not been tested since Bud Ewing's last adjustments. The affect obviously confused the Russian pilots and their radar operators. The reports were now of not one, but six unidentified aircraft crossing the Bering Strait. Alex looked below and saw the lower clouds had dissipated and the pack ice of the strait was visible beneath their aircraft. Above him were the lights of several jets obviously searching for the Eagle in the darkness.

The Diomede Islands were just 30 miles away. Once he was beyond these, the Eagle would be in American airspace. All four occupants of the plane were straining in their seats as they peered through their windows at the approaching MIGs. They could only hope the aircraft had not been spotted and the MIG pilots were busy chasing the make-believe targets. Alex had no way of knowing the technicians in Moscow had unraveled the mystery of the displacement of the disponder, allowing them to zero in on the actual location of the aircraft. The fact Alex had set the disponder to display six targets instead of three would keep them busy just a little while longer, but no doubt they would crack the code. Thirty miles, twenty-eight now, just eight minutes. Could they make it or would they wind up a twisted hunk of plastic and flesh on the pack ice below? There was no skill involved. Alex knew they had to rely on the darkness, the disponder and luck if they were to make it to America. Karen knew of a higher power working in their favor as she silently prayed for divine protection.

Each minute seemed to stretch into ten. Alex felt as if the tailwind had shifted and was now a 200 knot headwind causing them to sit still in the Soviet Airspace. He had no idea how many Russian jets were out there, but he wouldn't have been surprised if they ran right into one, they were so numerous. Lights appeared below them. Was it one of the islands, or a freighter breaking its way through the ice? Suddenly, up ahead they saw two jets approaching from the east. Alex and Karen in the front seats of the Eagle held their breath. These two jets were coming close. Above the din they heard a voice on the radio. It came across, clear and deep, in English. "Welcome home, Eagle. J. L. and Susan send their regards."

Alex and Karen looked at each other in surprise. The jets were American! Karen began beating Alex on the shoulder, laughing and crying at the same time. Alex was doing all he could to ward off her ecstatic blows and fly the airplane. The voice came through again, "Have a good flight to Nome, Sir. We'll entertain your escort for you." Alex, Karen, Lev and Dmitri Flerov all turned in their seats to witness the MIGs turning back toward the west with the American F-15's hot on their tails. Even Flerov seemed to be impressed.

Then it hit Alex and Karen at the same time and they turned slowly toward each other with disbelief. "Did he say J. L. and Susan?" Alex asked.

Thirty-five minutes later, Alex taxied the Windecker Eagle up in front of the hangar at Nome Airport, the one where he had arranged to have the Eagle painted just a little more than a week earlier. As the propeller slowed to a stop, Karen opened the door on her side of the airplane. The hangar door in front of them slid open. Inside, in the dim light, the Eagle's passengers could just barely make out three familiar figures. Alex, for one, couldn't wait to get out of the airplane and into the arms of one of those people waiting in the hangar. He climbed off the wing and ran into Susan's arms. "What are you doing here?" he asked as he literally swept her off her feet. She was crying tears of joy, but finally managed to answer.

"It was Mr. McDaniels," she answered, "He brought me here. He knew you would be coming in sometime tonight."

"Oh, really?" Alex said, turning to McDaniels with Susan hanging onto his arm. "I want to talk to you about that." As Karen joined them, Susan reached out and hugged her. "In the morning, Alex," J. L. answered. "We'll have plenty of time to talk about it. Meanwhile, we've got you all some accommodations downtown at the hotel. Let's all go get some sleep."

"Sleep!" Karen said. "I'm starving. Where can you get steak and potatoes this time of night?"

McDaniels laughed, "I know a place right downtown. Come on, let's go."

The other person with Susan and McDaniels was Bud Ewing. McDaniels had brought him into what was going on and Bud had come along to help get the Eagle back to Texas. He had been instrumental in helping the U.S. Air Force locate the Eagle when it had come across the strait with the MIGs in hot pursuit.

On the way to the restaurant, Alex and Karen introduced Dr. Orgutsov and Dmitri Flerov to the others. Flerov was quiet, but no trouble. He was just taking everything in, watching the freedom with which the Americans expressed and entertained themselves. He was comfortable with the English language, and could follow the conversations easily. Dr. Orgutsov was not so fortunate. He was jovial, but Alex had to translate nearly everything for him that was said.

Later, after the steaks had been ordered, the seven sat around a table in the dining room of the Nome Nugget Inn. Alex was full of questions he wanted answered. "J. L.," Alex said. "I used to be pretty good at both sending and recognizing subliminal messages when I worked for the agency. I thought I knew all the tricks, but you really got me on this one."

"What are you talking about, Alex?" McDaniels asked.

"I want you to tell me how you managed to get to me with the subliminal messages that convinced me to do this mission," Alex said.

"Alex," J. L. began, "The first time I knew you were up to something was when the KGB started inquiring about you. Somebody was trying to find out about you and they wanted information fast. They got a little careless. I picked up on it and found out you had disappeared. The KGB was real interested in your friend, Karen, too. I started doing a little checking myself and found out she was in the Soviet Union. Then our guys over there started picking up on some strange activities and they all seemed to point to the fact you were up to something. It took me the better part of three days to put enough pieces together for me to begin to figure out what you were up to. I wasn't sure it was Orgutsov, but I was beginning to suspect it. Our friend Flerov here was a complete surprise to me."

Alex laughed, "He was a surprise to me as well, and to himself. What about it Dmitri? What do you make of all of this?"

Flerov hesitated a moment before speaking. As he spoke, Alex translated for Dr. Orgutsov. "I have always aspired to be a man of adventure. For me, the KGB offered the best opportunity for action. Throughout my career, I have been gravely disappointed. It seems the rewards have always gone to the ones who have been politically conniving. I am intelligent, yet I have not been so astute as some of my peers. I had come to believe there was no real adventure within the Soviet Union. There have been only repeated disappointments and empty promises of rewards that are to come sometime in the future. Tonight I am a lonely man. You are rejoined with your friends and loved ones while my family is far away. Yet I feel for the first time in my life I have the opportunity to find adventure. I may wind up in an American prison, but I hope I can be of more value than that."

"Certainly you will," J. L. assured him. "My government will want to learn many things from you, but I assure you, you will be a free man."

"What about my family?" Flerov asked. "Is there really a chance you can get them to America?"

McDaniels smiled at the question. "Ask our friend Mr. Davis here. He seems to be an expert at getting that type of mission accomplished. What about you, Dr. Orgutsov? What made you want to come to America?"

"Yes," Alex added as he translated J. L.'s question. "If CAFI didn't set this all up, what caused you to approach Karen, and where did you get the idea of coming to America?"

There was a pause before the doctor answered, as the waitress brought the steaks to the table. The two Russians seemed to be in awe of the type of service that could be provided at an American restaurant at two o'clock in the morning. They obviously were not used to the idea of walking into a place and ordering such a meal at this time of night. The two men dug into their steaks eagerly.

"I have always had the desire to teach," Dr. Orgutsov explained. "It has been a theory of mine that those of us who possess knowledge owe it to others to share that knowledge. Unfortunately, my theory is not very well thought of in the Soviet Union. When I listened to Dr. Webster in Moscow, I observed she was what I desired to be—a gifted teacher. In fact, she imparted the knowledge she had with a type of enthusiasm I coveted. From the first time I saw her, I began formulating a plan that would get the knowledge I had learned about how to cure cancer to her so she could teach it to others. The idea of coming here to America myself seemed preposterous, yet I secretly desired it and I apparently let my desires be known to the right person, at the right time."

Initially, there was silence around the table as Alex translated Dr. Orgutsov's explanation. It was Susan Davis who finally broke the silence. "Do you mean, Alex, you did this entire thing because you thought CAFI wanted you to, and the fact is CAFI didn't even know about it until you were already in Russia?"

"That's apparently right, Susan," McDaniels took it upon himself to answer.

Alex added, "The circumstances came together so well, I just knew they had to have been orchestrated. I even thought you were behind Karen's initial trip to Moscow, J. L."

"Didn't know a thing about it, Alex," McDaniels answered. "You must have been ripe for the plucking."

"I'll say," Susan chimed in. "Alex had been moping around the house feeling useless for months. I think he psychologically needed something like this to keep him from thinking he was growing old."

"Old!" Karen exclaimed. "There you go again. Alex is the same age as I am, and I am not old! I don't want to hear anymore of that kind of talk."

Later in their hotel room, Alex confided in Susan, "Honey, I wanted to tell you what was going on, but I believed knowing about CAFI would be detrimental to you."

"Alex, I have known about CAFI since before we were married," Susan told him. "I didn't know what you were up to this time, and for a while I even started to think you had run off with Karen."

"Run off with Karen?" Alex was puzzled. "What would I want to do that for? You're the one I married. Karen is like family, like a sister. You know that."

"I know. It was silly. But sometimes your imagination plays tricks on you. And you were being so mysterious and no one knew where you were and no one knew where Karen was and, you know ...."

"Now can we turn off the light?" Alex asked.

"Okay," Susan said. "But Alex, I hope you realize this whole thing *was* orchestrated by someone and I know He protected all of you and made it possible for you to come back safely. He sure had me praying a lot for you."

Alex looked at her. "You're right. It had to have been God," he said. "How could I have been so blind all these years to what you and Karen have been telling me about how God works in our lives?" Susan smiled. She knew they would have more conversations about God in the future and it would no longer be a closed door.

In her room two doors down, Karen sat on the edge of her bed. She was still feeling the excitement from their recent adventure, especially the chase. She closed her eyes and again visualized the two American fighters coming toward the Eagle in the darkness and the voice on the radio welcoming them home. Karen decided she liked that kind of adventure. It was no wonder Alex had taken up CAFI's offer years before and he had so easily been persuaded to try this mission. Karen knew she would do it all over again, given the chance. She smiled as she turned out the light and pulled up the cover. It would be a while before she was relaxed enough to go to sleep.

Four hundred miles to the west, Colonel Veektor Zhukov, KGB, stood among the burned wreckage of a Soviet helicopter. His own aircraft had been just five kilometers behind this one when the missile from the MIG had blown it to bits. The American agent, Alex Davis, had been extremely fortunate to have escaped. Zhukov would have a lot of explaining to do to his superiors. The one thing that would be the most difficult to explain would be the disappearance of Dmitri Flerov. Flerov had forced his MIG pilot to land at the small airstrip at Nerpichiy and had apparently flown away from there with the American. It certainly seemed that Alex Davis had been helped by someone. Had Flerov been an American spy right under his own nose? Surely not, yet it seemed to be the only logical explanation for what had happened. Oh, well, Zhukov thought as he shrugged his shoulders. At least I can use him as a scapegoat for my own failures. With that, he walked away into the night.

Also by David Freeman

Highways in the Sky
Oxpatch and the Hill
Nam Rescue

Available at nissibooks.com